THIS THING (

This Thing of Darkness

Heathcliff's Lost Years

Nicola Edwards

Aderyn

First published in Great Britain in 2023 by Aderyn Press
Gweledfa, Felindre, Swansea, Wales, SA5 7NA

www.aderynpress.com

A CIP catalogue record for this book is available from the British
Library

ISBN 978-1-9163986-8-9
eISBN 978-1-9163986-9-6

Cover design: Kari Brownlie
Text design: Elaine Sharples
Printed in Great Britain by 4edge Ltd

'This thing of darkness,
I acknowledge mine.' – The Tempest, Shakespeare

For Glyn and Arthur, with love.

Abe Earnshaw

Gimmerton, Yorkshire

July 1771

'We will rest there a while,' I said, pointing to Gimmerton in the valley below.

The boy looked up at me and cocked his head slightly, like an intelligent dog trying to find meaning in its master's words.

'Don't you worry, lad,' I said, placing my hand on the boy's shoulder. 'You'll soon learn the language – finest *Yorkshire* English.'

Dusk was nearly upon us, but the valley was all damson purple and leaf green, despite the dimming light. I pointed again to where the valley narrowed and then broadened, to the clutch of stone dwellings, and beyond, deep within the vale's furrow, Gimmerton. I am always thankful to return to this dale after a long journey, to return to the smoke that rises from the village, an exhalation at the end of a long day.

'It isn't Liverpool,' I said, pulling the boy close to me, out of the wind. 'But there's a fine inn, and the innkeeper is a goodly man.'

Holding the boy close, I began our descent to the village, along a path bordered with brambles and dense patches of heather. My legs and arms gnawed in protest. It had been a long walk from Liverpool, and I was bone tired.

'I'm getting too old for this,' I said.

The boy clung to my waist.

'You run ahead,' I said, gently pushing him forward.

The wind funnelled through the combe and swept the curls from the boy's face. His eyes were dark, darker than any of the Earnshaws, but they were also deep and serious and not unfamiliar.

I watched him closely as the thickets came alive. Black grouse gurgled and shrieked amongst the bracken. Skylark called to one another. A buzzard screeched above. The boy crouched low and tilted his head.

'Don't be afraid,' I said as gently as I could, lifting the boy to his feet despite my soreness. 'These moors are filled with noises; soon you will learn to name them all, even mimic them. Cathy will teach you; she can trill like a skylark, when it pleases her,' I said, thinking of my wayward daughter. 'You will like Nelly, our house girl,' I said. 'She will do you no harm.'

The boy stayed close to me as dusk swept into the hills and moorland. One by one the candles were lit; they flickered like stars in the cottage windows. As more chimneys began to smoke, the smell of burning wood filled the valley. I had not known the comfort of a good fire since leaving the Heights three days hence.

'Do you smell that, lad?'

The boy looked at me blankly.

'Like this,' I said, lifting my chin and smelling the air elaborately.

The boy copied me, but still looked confused.

'It is fire,' I said, using my hands to replicate the movement of flames. 'Resting before a good hearth is a joy like no other.'

The boy nodded, his expression serious, but then I smiled at him, and the boy's features softened. His smile, when it came, was too big for his face.

'Come here, lad,' I said, kneeling before him so our faces were level. I was unsteady and the wind nearly felled me.

I gestured for the boy to come closer.

I cradled the back of the boy's neck, and the boy did not flinch at my touch. Instead, he leaned into my hand, and closed his eyes.

My breath snagged in my chest. I was a child again, soothed by the touch of my own father's hand.

The boy opened his eyes to a tenderness I could not conceal.

'You are my son,' I said.

Soon I would weave my lies to the village, to my wife, to Cathy and Hindley, even to the boy. But not yet.

'You are my son,' I repeated, still holding the boy's neck, not wanting the warmth to fade, as I knew it must.

Robert Feather

The Black Bull Inn, Gimmerton
September 1780

I first set eyes on him when he was a bairn, carried to the Heights by old Earnshaw after one of his jaunts. Brazen he was, bringing the lad here and setting him down on a stool near the fire for all to gawp at. The boy was dark, darker than pitch, and I wasn't sure if it was dirt that clung to him or the devil.

'Feather, I've a thirst that could drain an ocean,' old Earnshaw called out. And when I looked at him in earnest, I saw that he was famished.

'Just got back, have you?' I asked, handing him a jug of ale, and scattering the silence that had just fallen like night.

Earnshaw glanced coldly at the other men in the inn. The saddler turned to resume his talk with his apprentice. One of Earnshaw's tenant farmers shuffled nearer to his pitcher and did a bad show of someone not listening. The other two men stared with intent at the boy. He must have sensed it, for he slipped off the stool and sat at Earnshaw's feet.

'Aye,' Earnshaw said, placing his hand on the boy's head as you would a dog, 'just now.' And then he raised his voice so that the men stopped jabbering and stared more keenly at their ale. Earnshaw was a landowner, and not to be nettled.

'I found this poor bairn on the streets of Liverpool. I didn't have the heart to leave him there to starve.' He picked up the boy and held him up. 'Look at the poor bairn. Could *you* leave him to his fate?'

He seemed to be speaking to the stirrings of suspicion within all of us, and I can't speak for those present that night, but I was shamed by my aversion to the lad. He *was* pitiable, even then, with rags for boots and hair so matted and long he could have been a lass, but there was something in his look as he glared from underneath those dark locks that made me think he wasn't as forlorn as Earnshaw had made known. His eyes were as hard as basalt, and his mouth seemed to chew on sounds only to swallow them whole. He was a silent, watchful thing, and plainly not a native of these parts.

'Does it not speak?' I asked.

Old Earnshaw glared at me, and I felt myself redden.

'*He* speaks from morning to evening ... but I confess it is gibberish to me,' Earnshaw said, setting the lad back on the stool. 'But he is no moon-calf. In time, his English will be vastly superior to yours, Feather, I assure you.'

'I'll fetch you another ale,' I said, scolded and eager to return to the familiar rhythms of the inn.

'Bring water for the lad, Feather,' he said, setting the boy on his knee. 'It has been an arduous journey and we've not reached the end of it yet.'

I collected the empty pitchers and was about to fetch water when the creak of floorboards above made me stop in dread. I dropped the pitchers on the counter and made for the stairs, but I was too late. Anne had already appeared, like an apparition, on the stairwell.

'What are you doing out of bed, wife?' I asked, placing a hand on her shoulder. 'You know what Doctor Kenneth said: you need rest.'

I noticed her pallor and unkept hair and attempted to steer her back up the stairs, but then she saw the lad, and she shrugged my hand away.

She walked slowly to old Earnshaw, crouching low so that she was closer to the lad's height. I knew what seeing the bairn would do to her, having lost ours not four week before, but I didn't want a row in front of our patrons, so I did not hinder her. I knew she noticed neither his rags nor his darkness; to her, he was a bairn in need of a mother.

'Hello,' she said, kneeling unsteadily before him.

We all watched to see if the boy would speak, but he merely studied her and made not a sound.

'I'm Mrs Feather,' she said softly. 'What is your name?'

'He has no name,' old Earnshaw answered. 'Not yet. But I fancy Heathcliff, the name of the son we lost.'

'Heathcliff, Heath-cliff,' she repeated, separating the word, sounding it out. 'A cliff of heathland,' she said absently, her mind off wandering again.

Old Earnshaw's features softened into something resembling pity. He gently pushed the lad towards Anne, and he did not protest.

She reached for him and held him close, and grief rose within me like a sickness.

'He is a gift from God, Mr Earnshaw,' she said, releasing the lad. 'My boy is in the ground, like your Heathcliff. I worry that my boy is cold down there in the damp and in the dark.'

'Go upstairs now,' I said quietly, fearful of betraying the grief that still held me in its grip.

I lifted her to her feet. Anne suddenly seemed to realise where she was and lowered her gaze when she became aware of the numerous eyes in the room. Gimmerton men are known to be free with their tongues, and I did not want her to be the subject of their idle talk.

She walked stiffly past me and up the stairs, where I knew, if I hadn't followed and shut the door behind her, the entire inn would hear her wretchedness.

She took an interest in the lad from then on; an interest I now wish I'd put a stop to. But who can predict these things except the Almighty? And He never uttered a word of warning.

It was on account of his power over Anne that the last time I saw him, some nine year later, on the night of that terrible storm folk still talk about, I was not well-pleased by his presence.

He burst through the door with the wind and the rain and the lightning at his back and surveyed the room from under those black brows. There were only two other souls here that night, the only men in Gimmerton foolhardy enough to venture out, and they paid him no heed as he pushed the door shut and skulked to one of the darker corners of the inn.

'Heathcliff,' I said. 'What brings you here at this hour and in this weather?'

He scowled at me, as was his custom, for in recent times he was generally of an unsociable disposition. The lad had lost his sullenness for a time, but after old Earnshaw's passing, Hindley Earnshaw had not looked kindly on his adopted brother. I could not blame him. Heathcliff could be as crooked as hawthorn and just as hardy.

'Heathcliff?' I pressed gently.

But he retreated further into his corner, and unease swelled in my chest. I knew there was something amiss that evening. Heathcliff was more unforthcoming than usual, but I kept at my work and tried to disregard the storm gathering in the recess. There was much to fret about at the inn that night. The Almighty had summoned a gale so lamentable that the old building creaked and groaned as though on a ferocious sea. Candles flickered in the wind that curled down the chimney and the quivering fire in the hearth flung fiendish shadows on all the walls. I was nervous, I must confess. When my only two patrons thought better of being away from home on such an evening and gathered their coats, I was left in the half-light with Heathcliff: an unenviable position even on a peaceful night. I resolved to be rid of him, and quickly. I did not want Anne bothered.

'You should be making your way back to the Heights, Heathcliff, or if I know Joseph, the doors will be locked and then what will you do?'

'Joseph can go to hell with his infernal righteousness. What do I care if he bolts the door? One day I shall smear his and Hindley's blood over the Heights until the stones are eternally red.' He leant forward in a fit of passion and I saw, in the blinking candlelight, the state he was in. His eyes had retreated even further under his brows and had become caverns fit for fiends. He was smeared in dirt, as though he'd flung himself from the Heights and stumbled his way down to Gimmerton.

His manner of clasping his arms, to prevent himself from lashing out I reckoned, made me pity him. He was just a lad at bottom, and a homeless one at that.

'Have you run away, Heathcliff?' I ventured.

'It has nowt to do with you.'

'I'm closing up,' I said, irked by his scorn. 'The storm has affrighted all God-fearing folk away; it's time for you to leave.'

'I'm not going until I speak with your missus,' he stated, gripping the table before him. I think I sighed, for I knew I could not move him any more than I could move the ground beneath.

'Don't be difficult lad. Mrs Feather is in bed,' I said, attempting to stand firm. 'I won't be disturbing her.'

'I need to see her,' Heathcliff said after a moment, his eyes glassy, but within seconds his expression was set, a frown cleaving his forehead. 'You *will* disturb her, or *I* will disturb *you.*'

I had a fancy to laugh, to heap scorn onto him, and then call for the magistrate, but I did not want Anne awakened. Her partiality for the lad was a weakness I never managed to master, much to my dismay.

It began the moment Heathcliff was old enough to roam.

Old Earnshaw would ride to Gimmerton with the lad holding on to his coat, smiling at folk and making Heathcliff's existence known to all. Earnshaw was proud of him, that much was evident, despite, or perhaps in answer to, the talk in the village.

There was a great deal of talk in them days.

Newcomers were rare and treated with suspicion, so my patrons were garrulous when it came to Heathcliff. I am not a gossip, a man's business is his own, but they fashioned a past for the lad that would have maddened old Earnshaw if he had heard of it, and so the lad's suspected origins were whispered just out of Earnshaw's hearing. It was known he would not tolerate a bad word said against the lad, and to my chagrin, neither would Anne.

She took to Heathcliff in a way I had not seen since our bairn breathed his last. I understood her fondness at first, it seemed natural, but Heathcliff was not a bonny lad, even as a bairn, and in recent times my heart had hardened towards him. To me he was a blackguard, rough-hewed in some devil's workshop to bring to nowt the fortunes of honest folk. To Anne he was always the 'poor orphan bairn', even when he had long ceased being a bairn. When old Earnshaw was alive, I could sway Anne, but after he died and Heathcliff became inured to ill-treatment, she kept the lad even closer.

Now, nine year later, he stood over me with his fists clenched. I did not want a fuss. The inn seemed to reel in the heavenly tumult outside and I am not ashamed to admit that I was unnerved by it.

'Set down, Heathcliff,' I said, as casually as I could muster. 'I'll get you a drink and you can tell me what has befallen you.'

'I must be gone presently,' he said, stepping so close I could smell the damp in his woollen jacket. 'Fetch your wife or be damned, Feather.'

When I did not move, Heathcliff made to dislodge me and venture upstairs himself. His conduct reeked of desperation, so I barred his way with a poker from the fire. The point flared in his coal-black eyes.

'Now what do we do, Heathcliff?'

I was in terror, and I was sure he could hear it in my voice, but the fight I had feared did not come. Perhaps he did not have the stomach for it or thought I was in earnest, but his eyes watered away the red gleam of the poker, and he was a lad again. He subsided onto a stool and covered his face with his hands, but I kept hold of the poker. All beasts are a danger, even when subdued.

'What has happened, Heathcliff?' I asked, keeping my distance. I considered the state he was in and his earlier remark, that he would 'be gone presently'; it gave me a hope I had never dared give thought to – that we could be rid of him, and Anne would come back to me.

I lowered the poker slightly and moved a step closer to him. 'Heathcliff? Are you leaving Gimmerton?'

He did not answer straightway but continued to sit masking his face. I noticed his fingers: dry crags with sediments of dirt for nails. I had heard much of Hindley's unkindness to him, and the proof was in his hands. The housekeeper at the Heights, Nelly Dean, had long been lamenting Hindley's treatment of a lad that was once set up as a rival for his father's affections. Every market day she would report on the goings-on up at the Heights, so us villagers had a fair idea of the ins and outs of things. Hindley was a sot after the passing of his wife and had reduced Heathcliff to a drudge. Hindley's bairn was blamed for her passing and was mistreated for it: I thanked the Almighty that Anne had not crossed *his* path. As for the comely Miss Catherine Earnshaw, she was mingling with the Lintons of Thrushcross Grange and who could blame the lass?

'Has Hindley forsaken you?' I asked, trying to ascertain his plans.

The mention of his persecutor produced a strange effect on him. I was sure, when he lifted his head, that he had been weeping, but there was a terrible ferocity behind his tears.

'Nay, not merely Hindley,' he said coldly. 'But I shall revenge myself on him soon enough.'

He stood, straightened his back, and seemed to recover some of his former boldness. I retreated and raised the poker again.

'I will not harass you, Feather, but nor will I leave,' he said, before pausing as though considering his next words carefully. He closed his eyes and nodded as though coming to a decision.

I stood silently and waited.

'Wake your missus,' he began, 'or I will stay until morning and declare from the steps of that infernal church *all* my relations with Mrs Feather,' he blasphemed, pointing to where the church of St Michael stood firm against the storm. 'You know me,' he warned. 'I shall do it.'

My mind flittered like a small bird in one of them cages Anne always wanted. I knew of the closeness between he and my wife, as I have already said, but I had not guessed the range of it. Something was amiss and although Heathcliff was to blame for Anne's state, I could not trust his word any more than I could the word of the devil.

'What relations would you have me believe, Heathcliff?' I asked, somewhat flayed by what he might utter and still gripping the poker.

I expected him to fly at me, but unlike afore, he smiled in defiance of his almost dry tears and drew a chair towards him. He used the stool from earlier as a footrest. Dry mud flaked from his boots, and I couldn't help watching it fall like leaves in autumn.

'Of the unspoken sort, not the sort to be set forth on the church steps,' he said, bringing my attention back to his words. He leaned back in his chair, feigning bluster I was sure of it, and added, 'I'm sure you would not want everyone from the blacksmith to the good Reverend to hear how you are a cuckold.'

He spoke the last few words very slowly, by design, but I did not hasten towards him with the poker. I was struck by a thought, a memory of something Nelly Dean, the housekeeper up at the Heights, had said in the years before old Earnshaw's passing: that Heathcliff was a cuckoo in the nest.

I was seized by doubt, and Heathcliff's false laughter as I backed towards the stairs made my blood beat against my skull like a thrush against its anvil. His slur dimmed my judgement and I resolved to wake Anne, despite my instincts, for I had questions for her; questions that had long been preying on my mind in our cheerless state.

'Very well, I will wake her,' I said, turning to take the stairs up to our lodging. 'But what would you have with her?'

He paused again, as though deciding which Heathcliff to perform in this instance. Eventually, with his head lowered, he settled on, 'I ... wish to say goodbye to her.' He uttered these words with a softness akin to affection, but then he shook his head, and his voice hardened. 'And what she owes me. I will not leave without it.'

I suddenly felt weary and suffered each moment as it passed by, but after regarding each other in silence for some time, I came to a resolution. I would speak with Anne if I found her in a reasonable state.

I took a candlestick, one of the few still lit, to aid my way up the stairs. When I glanced back at Heathcliff, he was curtained in near darkness, a spectre in the recess. I made a silent prayer to the Almighty and turned towards the stairs to our living quarters.

The steps to Anne's room groaned underfoot, and the higher I climbed the more the storm vexed me. It was unseasonable for September. Lightning is not unheard of in these parts, but the gales that shook the inn that night are seldom seen before Michaelmas. I can never sleep when the elements rage, but Anne would slumber even if fire licked the canopy of the bed and set the drapes aflame. I should have seen the storm as a warning from the Almighty, that something diabolical was fore-doomed to ride the wind into my inn.

I had no notion of how the evening would end, but I was angry at Anne for her imagined transgressions and for admitting Heathcliff into our life. The Almighty was not to blame for the canker she had nourished for many a year.

I stood outside her chamber for a moment before edging open the door. I could not be rid of the pictures laiking in my mind; loathly images summoned by Heathcliff to plague me. I thought of our old nights together in the cold bed that was once warm, and I am ashamed to admit that I began to trust Heathcliff's slander against my wife. In my choler I thought perhaps the devil could speak true. I clenched my fist around the poker that I was surprised to still be holding and entered the chamber.

The room was dark and biting cold. The curtains did nowt to keep the draught out and were swollen with the wind's breath. I said that Anne could sleep through any bother, and in that dreary room I saw the proof of it. Even without the aid of the candle, I knew the drapes were loose and that Anne slept with the blanket at her feet despite the chill. I knew she wore a nightgown soiled with sweat and worse besides and that I would wash it anew in the morning. It was the same nearly every night since Heathcliff was old enough and sly enough to ill-use her for his own ends. I reckoned I could strike her with the poker and still she would slumber. I am not proud of my thoughts that night, or the way I set the candlestick too close to the drapes and prodded her empty belly with the end of the poker. She lay in the bed our bairn was born in, where he slept before the Almighty saw fit to take him. It was a bed we had not shared for nearly five year.

Anne was a winsome woman of twenty-seven when we wed. My first wife was a cant, slip of a lass and perished of consumption not two year after the wedding. I hoped Anne would be hardier, and she was in some ways. She was hale enough to withstand birthing and the bairn's passing wasn't her doing. Doctor Kenneth said she would be herself again and gave her laudanum to hasten her recovery. Nine year on, Kenneth had long ceased issuing comfort and Anne had long learnt to find it elsewhere. It gave her a relief I could not bestow so I thought nowt of it for many a year. It was her regard for Heathcliff that first alerted me she was in the grip of a terrible sickness.

At first, she would seek him out, attending to him while old Earnshaw went about his business in Gimmerton. She would comb the knots from his hair and then take him out to the stables to show him the horses. I grew used to seeing the lad in the inn and I was not averse to his presence; he had an interest in the workings of the inn, and for a time he seemed to bring Anne back to life. Then folk began to talk, with pity, about 'poor barren Mrs Feather', replacing her dead bairn with a 'foreigner'.

I had no way of knowing if she was barren, since relations between us had ceased and I am not a cruel man. But at that point in time, she was not lost to me. She still had a bloom in her cheeks and a pleasing figure that proved a torment to me in those hours before sleep when we still made a show of sharing a bed.

The thought of what she once was made me lay the poker aside and set down on the edge of the bed. Anne was feverish as always and her greying hair, like wet leaves, stuck to her forehead. Her eyes were hollow, and her cheeks were as lined as limestone.

I cursed myself for my weakness. I was no cuckhold. She had feelings for Heathcliff, but they weren't of that sort. How could they be? She was as worn and as cold as a crag.

The sudden screech of a chair being pushed back downstairs startled me, thence I did not perceive that Anne was awake until I felt her hands on mine.

'Robert? Is that you?' she murmured, straining her eyes. 'What are you doing?'

'Nowt,' I said quickly, hiding the poker behind me and raising the blanket so that it covered her legs. 'I was worried you might be cold.'

She kicked the blanket away and heaved her body over the edge of the bed.

All was silent again below.

'Nay, Anne. You must not take any more,' I said, holding onto her despite her stale stench.

But she was possessed of some devil's strength, and I couldn't hinder her. She reached over the side and groped in the darkness beneath the bed. I heard the clamour of glass and then two bottles rolled from my wife's dispensary. She blindly reached for one, shook it and threw it aside in agitation. It hit the wall but did not shatter. I hoped the sound was lost in the swell of the storm, but it led to more movement below and I was overcome with a dread of seeing Heathcliff looming in the doorway like

17

a rook. Anne had no notion of my disquietude and had righted herself on the bed, gripping the second bottle. She lifted it to her lips and drank it empty. After a moment, her entire body shivered, and she let out a sigh that was piteous to hear.

'Anne?' I said, venturing closer to her.

She stared past me at the quivering shadows cast by the candle I had brought with me. It was near smothered by the wind that issued from the window and I had a fear of being in darkness whilst Heathcliff was free to roam the inn.

'Anne?' I said once more, smoothing her damp hair, all the while listening for Heathcliff.

She gazed at me then with such a countenance of despair that I thought my heart would crack like a sparrow's egg.

'I have no more, Robert. You must fetch Heathcliff and tell him,' she said, pleading. I glanced my eye at the door once more; the devil is known to appear when he is summoned.

'I have money,' she said, turning and fumbling with a drawer in her bedside table.

'Hold still, lass,' I said, stroking her hand until she was tranquil.

I knew where she found the means to pay Heathcliff for the laudanum and I feared I was answerable for her dependence on that ungodly vagabond and the opium he supplied. I did nowt to stop her and paid no heed to her descent into slothfulness or the shillings that went astray every market day. I was banished from the marriage bed and did nowt to reclaim it. The reverend advised me to take her in hand, but I confess to not knowing how.

'You must sleep, Anne. I should not have awoken you,' I said, standing with the intent to leave.

She hung her head and lay down once more, but instead of feeling glad of her mildness, I was in a state of agitation and feared how the evening would conclude. She loved Heathcliff; I was sure of it. She loved him with the blind partiality of a mother. Would she ever forgive me if she knew I'd concealed his presence from her, on what would become his final evening in Gimmerton? I decided, for right or wrong, that she would not find out.

I slowly reached into the drawer she had left ajar. I found no money but that was not my intent. I groped for the key that was always kept there and swathed it in my hand.

'Good night, Anne,' I said, picking up the candlestick and backing out of the room. Her eyes were staring, and she was deathly pale.

It wasn't the first time I had locked her in that chamber, and it wasn't fated to be the last. I shut the door gently and I was comforted by the click of the lock as I made fast the room. I listened at the door for a moment and when I was satisfied all was calm, I turned to descend the stairs.

I heard nowt from Heathcliff, so I did not hasten. I only had a scant amount of time to settle on a plan. I stood at the top of the stairs for some moments, watching the ripples of candle-light on the walls. Heathcliff would need to be got rid of, that much was plain – and with no disturbance. All was quiet down-stairs and for an instant I entertained the hope that Heathcliff had departed of his own accord, back into the storm from whence he came. This hope carried me down the stairs, but it was extinguished even before I had set foot on the final step.

Heathcliff was standing at the window, gazing into the night. The curtains were undone, and they swelled around him.

'You cannot see the moors from here. I never noticed before,' he said soberly, and then with nowt but wonder, asked, 'How can you abide it?'

The floor was besprinkled with raindrops, and I perceived with a jolt that the window was wide open. I hastened to close it and saw that Heathcliff was near drowned.

'This is folly, lad,' I said, fastening the casement. 'You will catch your death,' I said, realising after the words were uttered that I meant them. He was young, at sixteen, and Anne was fond of him, but his ill-use of her, his abhorrent claim to know her intimately, his threat to voice that falsehood, I could not forgive. He was a lad in the process of re-making himself into something else, something unnatural.

'Nay, I will not die yet,' he said. 'Not until I settle my score with Hindley, for raising me so low. That's what Cathy said – we would be together if Hindley had not *raised me so low.*' He paused, before emitting through closed teeth, 'Hindley is to blame, and I shall make him suffer more than merely the loss of that brach he called wife.'

He uttered this speech with such bile that I was curious – I will not deny it – but I was too angry to become his intimate.

'Hindley was wrong to keep you close, Heathcliff. You are the wilderness at his door; is it any wonder he fastens it against you?'

'You're mad to speak so, Feather,' he said, taken aback. I searched for the poker; what a time to realise it was locked in Anne's room!

'Set down, Heathcliff, and we shall talk,' I said, calmly, gesturing to the chair he had habited when he emblazoned me a cuckold.

'Where is your missus? I heard movement above,' he said, tilting his head to the ceiling. 'Shall I fetch her for you, Feather? I am certain she would come down for *me.*'

'I know how you misused her. How you have a store of pounds and shillings hidden away. How did you keep it from Hindley?' I asked, struggling to keep my voice from breaking. 'But it is no matter. I am no cuckold. There is a sickness in Anne, and you are the blight.'

Heathcliff's eyes widened, in surprise I thought, but then his face hardened as a thought took flight and settled on him like a gadfly.

'Make haste, Feather, and fetch her, or I have told you where I shall be come morning.'

I thought of the benevolence Anne had shown him, of my many kindnesses to him, and suddenly all the anger and bitterness left me. If I was still in possession of the poker, I would have let it fall into Heathcliff's hands. *He* would know what to do with it.

'Tell me what you want, and I shall fetch it for you, if I can,' I said, staring at my useless hands. When I glanced my eye at Heathcliff, he was smiling, but not in triumph. I could not read him. I never could.

'I need all the money you have ready, a travelling coat and a horse,' he said, leaning forward. 'And then I'll be gone. I will not trouble you again.'

'You are already in possession of enough of my money, lad; enough to see you right for a spell. I cannot give you more. But a good travelling coat and a horse I can provide you with.'

Heathcliff considered my proposal a moment, and after a further glance towards the stairwell, silently nodded. I was relieved but did not want to yield to that relief lest he was laiking with me.

'Are we settled then, Heathcliff?' I asked, haltingly.

'Aye, Feather,' he said in a low voice.

His quietude unsettled me. Heathcliff was never an obliging lad and despite knowing him most of his life, I could not follow this latest turn in temperament. It was an older version of him, yet another side to him, but his eye lingered on the stairs so I suspected he still hoped to harass Anne.

'If you stray upstairs, I will be less obliging and call for assistance,' I said, tapping my pocket, making sure I was still in possession of the key to Anne's room.

'Nay, there is no need,' he said, and I was confounded, for the lad's eyes were wet.

I said nowt and went to fetch my travelling coat from the recess under the stairs. When I returned, he had composed himself.

'Take it,' I said, handing it to him. 'It may not fit you, but it is well-made and all I have.'

Heathcliff took the coat and held it in front of him, running his eye over the cut and gauging the quality of the rubber.

'It should withstand rain,' I said, and then realised my foolishness: I was not selling him the habit; he was taking it from me.

But once the coat was on him, he filled all the spaces I was too slight to occupy. It befitted him, therefore, I did not bemoan its loss. I looked at the lad and caught a glimpse of the man he would become: hard and forceful and at heart cruel, depending on what would befall him as he ventured into the world. I wondered where he was going, but I did not press him. I knew Anne would bother me for the circumstances of Heathcliff's flight, and the less I knew about his whereabouts the fewer lies I would need to tell.

'I'll take you to the stables,' I said simply, and led him through the back, past the larder and into the night and the wind and the rain.

We owned three horses then. They were kept in the stables behind the inn: two mares and a colt not four year old. He was a fine horse that I spent half a year's earnings on. The mares I used for lugging barrels and the like, but I had plans for the colt and once he was old enough, I reckoned on making my money back with interest. All the horses were restless that night. The storm had driven them to the corners of the stables and as I approached with Heathcliff, I could tell they were fretting. Their neighs filled the wind's pauses.

'Heathcliff, fetch the lantern!' I shouted above the elements and the cries of the horses. I looked up at Anne's window, for it overlooked the yard, and I thanked the Almighty she was not standing there to witness the strangeness of our conduct.

Heathcliff hastened into the inn and returned with the lantern I had asked for, his face contorted in its light. A few slates had fallen from the roof, and I was heedful to avoid stepping on them. Heathcliff, as he followed me to the stables, crushed one underfoot and I meditated on what had vexed the Almighty and if the storm would cease once Heathcliff was gone. There has not been a storm like it since, not even as a harbinger of Heathcliff's return three year later.

'This way,' I uttered, gesturing with my hand. He, of course, knew the way, but I was sodden and keen to bring the evening to an end.

I led him to one of the mares, the one I was least aggrieved about losing. She was not young but would still carry Heathcliff a safe distance. I was not certain she could carry him back, but I did not make this known to him. It was the horse he had taken to when he was a bairn.

The mare was bothered by the storm and the fire in the lantern. Her eyes were wide and wild with fear, so I entered the barn and tried to calm her with soothing sounds. The poor horse was cowering from the circles in the puddles as it rained through the holes in the thatched roof. Heathcliff watched from the door as I set down the lantern and lifted the saddle from its hook and collected the halter and bridle. I was weighing the cost of it all and how much I would lose when I realised Heathcliff was gone.

I dropped the horse tack, picked up the lantern and went back into the yard. I was shivering from the cold and getting more and more fretful, and then I heard the colt. I thought it was the storm again, battering a wall or crumbling a chimney, but then I knew it to be the sound of hooves striking wood and I had a fair idea of where Heathcliff had got to. I ran against the rain, wondering how I'd explain it to Anne if I found Heathcliff splayed on the floor. But I found him holding the colt's head and stroking him calm. He always had a way with horses, even when he was not much older than a bairn.

'I'll take this one,' he said, when my lantern cast the scene in light.

'You can't have that one,' I said.

'Fetch the track and get him ready,' he said, taking no notice of me.

I did not have the resolve or the hardiness for another quarrel, so I did what he asked.

When I am solitary, I brood over the happenings of that night. I alter the story, varying the outcome until I am contented. In some of my imaginings, Heathcliff never darkens my door and in others he is a benign being, sent from heaven to replace our lost bairn, rather than from hell, bent on ruining us. But my fancies cannot change the truth of that night or the nights that followed. Heathcliff's departure could not go unseen; I was a fool to think otherwise.

For when I returned with the tack, Anne was in the window above.

I shuddered, half from the cold wetness of my clothes but more from her ghostly appearance. I was, and still am, a God-fearing man, and I saw her form at the window as a herald of some ruination. Her nightgown hung on her, leaving one of her breasts bare, and her white face, as it loomed out of the darkness, was terrible to behold. I rushed into the colt's stable and threw the saddle at Heathcliff's feet.

'You must be gone now, Heathcliff. Make haste. Saddle the horse and I shall do the rest.'

The horse was strangely calm, as though Heathcliff had cast a spell on him. He took the halter with no trouble, and within moments, both the colt and Heathcliff were ready to depart. Heathcliff led the animal out to the yard, both their coats glistening under the lantern light. When Anne saw them, she beat her fists against the windowpanes until I was sure the glass would shatter.

'Begone, Heathcliff!' I shouted, my voice carried by some sudden gale.

Heathcliff climbed onto the colt and held the reins tight, so the horse was stationary. He looked up at Anne and she halted her assault on the windowpanes. She was a bird in a cage.

'Do not stop the laudanum at once,' Heathcliff said, hanging over me. 'Get the doctor to issue smaller amounts. You will kill her if you pay no heed to my words.'

He did not await my reply. He struck the colt with his boots and was gone, back into the night and away. I glanced at the window and Anne had receded from view.

I stood in the rain and fumbled with the key in my pocket until the beat of hooves faded into wind.

Ned Morgan

Liverpool

September 1780 – November 1781

After the third blow, he stayed down for longer than before, and what a blow it was. I thought the boy was dead, but then he slowly and stiffly raised himself until he was upstanding.

He'd left an imprint in the mud he'd been felled so hard.

I couldn't fathom why he held out, when most stay slunk in the mud and suffer the loss of their horse quietly. Instead, he tried to guard the animal and then spat blood in Ben Naylor's face, daring him. I tried to hide a smile; I knew Naylor's temperament and that the boy would not be getting up a fourth time. The onlookers seemed to sense what was coming and retreated into the inn. They knew the wisdom of looking the other way.

Naylor wiped the blood from his face and glanced in my direction with a look that said, don't fucking tell me to stop now, don't you dare. The pause allowed the boy a second to ready himself and, when I felt he was steady enough on his feet, I nodded at Naylor, who was like a bulldog straining on a leash. The boy seemed to notice me for the first time, now the crowd had scattered, and gave me a look of such hatred that I felt the impulse to laugh. I remember thinking that if he survived, I would find some use for him.

Naylor grinned at the boy and did an excitable little dance, moving from side to side with his elbows bent. The boy watched him with his one good eye; the other was clotted shut. He waited for Naylor to attack, and when he did strike, lashing his body one way and then another, the boy sidestepped him, stumbling slightly but avoiding the blows aimed at him. Naylor was rabid but, not for the first time that day, I thought the boy might have the mettle to hold sway.

As Naylor advanced on him, the boy stepped forward and punched him in the muzzle. Naylor took a step back and held his nose, which was bleeding freely. The boy could certainly look after himself, but that punch took all his remaining strength, and he knew it.

He edged towards the horse and would have mounted it despite his injuries, if Naylor hadn't got hold of his coat and pulled him to the ground. I caught Naylor's eye and inclined my head in the direction of the wall, where, waiting, was the plank of wood that had ended many a fight. The three rusted nails jutting out of the wood tended to settle matters forthwith.

Naylor kicked the boy in the stomach, right in the intestines, over and over, until he vomited onto the mud. He rested his head in it whilst Naylor went to fetch the board. The sound of the boy's choked gasps filled the silence, but he still used what strength was left in his arms to get up. I admired his fortitude, so I only allowed Naylor to hit him with the plank twice. Once on his back, so that the nails punctured his flesh, and the second on his head, so that blood streamed into his mouth and the boy lost all awareness. Then I reined Naylor in.

'Fucking black bastard,' he said, kicking him once more, in the ribs this time, before taking out his cock and pissing on the boy's head. 'Best way to wash the blood off,' Naylor explained, laughing but breathing hard.

That was over a year ago, and I feel no shame over what happened next. Heathcliff, as I now know him, didn't do too badly out of the beating, all things considered.

I sent a lad from the inn to Liverpool to fetch the gaoler, whilst I kept watch over Heathcliff. I was afeard he would awaken and flee, but he was still insensible when the gaoler arrived an hour later.

He was a short, sullen man and unfamiliar to me, so I spun my usual narrative.

'The boy tried to thieve my horse. I'm in Mr Naylor's debt, for if he had not intervened the colt would be gone, leaving me out of humour and out of pocket.'

'Did the lad deserve such a beating?' the gaoler asked, kneeling next to Heathcliff, feeling for a heartbeat.

'Yes, the boy is near dead, but he fought back, so what else could Mr Naylor do?' I asked, incredulous at the man's manner.

'Are there witnesses?' he asked, standing to face me.

'No. My word is currency enough,' I said, and after a pause, 'I am Edward Morgan. You might know me as *Ned* Morgan.'

The gaoler blanched at my name and gave way instantly. He ordered his men to lift Heathcliff onto the back of the gaol cart.

In the main I let them rot in the Tower, but I saw something in Heathcliff – a hardness akin to my own force of will. I would break that will and rebuild it in a form more serviceable to me.

'Lodge him in your most miserable quarters and send word to me when he awakes,' I said, and as an afterthought I added, 'beat him again once he is clear-headed enough to know where he is.'

Heathcliff was carried one way and Naylor led my new colt the other. He was a fine-looking horse and would make a goodly sum, but I would offer the horse back to Heathcliff once the Tower had crushed him and what remained of him belonged to me.

I left Heathcliff there for three days.

I had work to complete for my backer, Samuel Unsworth, and it took up much of my time. There were plans afoot for another shipwreck, hence much needed to be girded. Unsworth desired order above all else, and the last wreck had been an untidy affair. There had been some chance passengers on the *Fortune*, so we pounded their heads with rocks and held them under water until their legs ceased kicking. It was a disordered business and I had to appease Unsworth long into the night. I assured him there was no record of the men and they were safely planted in Crosby Sands.

Unsworth came round to my way of thinking, but it was a long and vexing evening. The customs men were the only people of importance in Liverpool he couldn't purchase, so I had to be more heedful of impediments in future wrecks. Unsworth was not a man to be gainsaid.

Heathcliff was not forgotten during those three days. He was merely less pressing than my other business. In truth, I expected him to either be dead or in the process of dying. I was in a strong position: if he lived, I would take him, and if he died, then I would have a fine horse to sell.

But when I arrived at the Tower, I found him very much alive.

There was barely a soul abroad that morning, for it was Sunday and they were all entombed in their churches. Water Street, with St Nicholas on one end and St George on the other, was unfrequented by its usual denizens, but they could be heard – the sailors in St Nicks and the merchants in St Georges, raising their voices in their selfsame hymns to a long-dead god. Give me the gaolhouse any day; you know where you are with the rough and the ripe, the wanton and the wrecked; there's none of this false virtue. For that reason, I relish the Tower on a Sunday. During those hours, when the inmates take their exercise, the Tower becomes a drab brothel. The chaplain watches over his flock as they fuck in the courtyard. Men with women, men with men, dirty with the dregs of the previous week's fornication, all to the peal of the Sunday bells. There is something liberating about men following their instincts freely, with no care for propriety, but on this Sunday morning I was too late; they were all locked away, out of sight.

I was escorted through the courtyard by Carter, my associate inside the Tower. He conducted me around the dunghills and chickens and into the east wing of the gaol.

'I sent for you three days ago to pick up the boy Naylor thrashed. Why did you send someone else?'

'My apologies, Mr Morgan. I was needed here,' he said. 'A female prisoner was beaten that day and died not long afterwards.'

'Beaten by another inmate or by your men?'

Carter considered me, but then his pitted face swelled into a smile. 'Come now, Mr Morgan, we don't want that Good Samaritan to return, writing reports, stirring unease.'

I remembered John Howard's visit and how unwelcome his

recommendations had been. He'd noted that the cells were inadequate, that the mixing of the sexes was an abomination and that the unsanitary conditions were a threat to the health of the inmates. The stench of shit did dominate the gaol, but I could think of Liverpool streets that reeked worse.

'How's the boy? Still alive?'

'Oh, yes. He spits and curses and kicks the other men away. We beat him, as you instructed.'

'Good. Has he become tame?'

'Not quite,' Carter said, grinning, his skin like orange peel in the clear morning light. He'd suffered from the pox as a young man.

'Well, take me to him,' I said, averting my eyes from the warden's face.

He led me into the armoury. For such a small gaol, they were in possession of enough weaponry to suppress a revolution – of the English sort at least. I took a musket from the rack and Carter chose a bludgeon, which was his usual weapon of choice.

'Is this loaded?' I asked, holding up the musket.

'Yes, but you might not need it. He's housed with a deserter and a thief. I think the deserter tried to get too close to the boy yesterday and paid the price. Neither of these men are violent, but the boy...'

'Yes,' I said, turning to leave the armoury. 'I have seen him take a beating and administer one; it's the reason for my interest in him. Has he revealed his name yet?'

'No, he has not spoken, except to curse,' he said, following me closely. 'The chaplain visited him this morning, on account of the boy's youth, but he did not find him very accommodating.'

We made our way purposefully across the courtyard to the north tower. The gaol seemed strangely subdued. The only sound came from the gulls that circled the courtyard, swooping from time to time to scavenge for something dropped or discarded, a piece of rotten meat or chicken feed. The birds circled overhead as Carter unlocked the door that led to the most inhospitable cells in the Tower, located deep within its bowels.

These cells, seven of them in all, were far underground and measly air filtered through narrow apertures in the doors. There was no light, no respite from the darkness and the wild imaginings of the inmates.

As we descended, Carter handed me a lantern but the flame, as we sank, grew faint. The air thinned, our shadows dispelled, and our footsteps echoed in that stone passageway like the tread of giants. But then the ground levelled and the fetor of trapped air, of twenty festering bodies, swallowed us and I fought the urge to turn back.

'He's in the last cell. This way, Mr Morgan,' Carter said, with his coat sleeve masking his nose and mouth.

The silence of the inmates was unsettling but also gratifying. There was no rattling of chains or pleads for clemency. They were subdued to their core. The Tower had worked its cruelty into the very bones of the prisoners, so I was in no doubt that Heathcliff's boldness would be blunted.

I was entirely mistaken, of course.

His cell was ten steps further underground and, as our footfalls grew quiet, I expected to hear movement within, but there was only the jangling of keys, the clink of metal against metal, and the final snap of the lock. The door groaned open, and we were struck by the stench of shit, piss, and a lifespan of sweat. The walls, in that tiny cell, seemed saturated with it. It was the perfect place to house the boy — that room would break a man twice his age.

Carter lifted the lantern so we could view the inmates. There were indeed three in all, and two averted their eyes from our light. They were chained to different walls. One of the prisoners, a man of middle age, recoiled against the far wall and twisted his body away from the lantern, which must have seemed like the sun to him. Heathcliff, with narrowed eyes, blinked away the darkness and peered at us. His skin was near black with dirt, and his hair was matted with dried blood.

'Do you know me, boy?' I asked.

When he did not answer, I moved closer, bending under the low ceiling.

'Do you know me, boy?' I asked again.

Heathcliff spat at my feet.

'Aye, I know you,' he said.

'I've come to claim you. What do you say to that?'

'You can go to the deuce. It is *my* horse, given to me not five day hence, and I will have nowt to do with you.'

'Come now,' I said. 'Your lies will be your undoing. Why would *you* be given a horse of that pedigree?'

He sighed deeply and fixed his eyes on the wall behind me.

I edged closer and was nearly overcome with the reek of him.

'Your trousers are filled with piss and shit,' I said, covering my nose with my sleeve.

'I like being dirty,' he said, his gaze still fastened on something beyond me.

I lowered my sleeve and smiled ruefully, playing the part of a philanthropist. 'What is your name? I cannot help you unless you are candid with me.'

He did not answer.

'What is your name?' I asked again, all patience.

'Answer him!' Carter intervened, striking him with the bludgeon. I motioned for Carter to refrain from beating him – an act we had played several times, and successfully. The other inhabitants of the cell began to bleat pathetically, but not Heathcliff. He was a rare individual, even then, and as hard as the Tower itself, calloused with suffering and trouble.

'I do not want to leave you here, boy, in this terrible place. But if you refuse to speak, then I will abandon you to Mr Carter's keeping. What will it be?'

Heathcliff examined the other inmates for a moment,

distasteful in their distress, and his features, which had briefly softened, deadened once more.

'Be gone,' he said. 'I will not speak with you.'

'Very well,' I said, sighing and shaking my head at Carter.

Carter motioned for me to leave the cell first, and whilst he secured the door, I tried to compose myself. I was not accustomed to dissent, and Heathcliff's rebuff did not sit well with me.

We did not speak until we were above ground.

'What do you intend to do?' Carter asked, once we were in the light and able to breathe more easily.

'Could I impose on your kindness for, say, a fortnight?' I asked.

'Of course,' he said, pausing briefly before continuing, 'although there is his board to consider. He will need food, of course, a change of clothes, other essentials.'

'I'll send Ben Naylor with a generous amount,' I said, knowing that Heathcliff would not benefit from any of it.

'Then I'm content for him to remain here.'

We walked on, crossing the courtyard, and scattering the gulls in a squall of feathers and shrieks. Still galled by Heathcliff's resistance, I decided on one of the birds, raised my musket and fired. The shot rebounded against the four walls of the gaol. Once the smoke had cleared, there was a perfectly white gull on the foul ground. There was very little blood; the bird could have merely dropped from the sky. Carter flinched when I handed him the musket, still hot.

'The boy needs to learn his place,' I said, slowly and with purpose. 'Move him into a cell with less placid prisoners. He needs his exercise, so he should be allowed to join the other men in the courtyard. He is such a hard bastard that I doubt he will need any assistance if, by chance, he is assaulted.'

'I understand you,' Carter said quickly.

'And for the love of fucking Christ, get this courtyard cleaned,' I said, crushing the gull's skull with my boot, grinding its brains into the stones.

The weeks that followed were tireless. Preparations were in hand for the piracy of Unsworth's vessel, the *Isabella*. It was a brave ship that had weathered many crossings from Jamaica but would soon be aged beyond use. On her final crossing, she would be carrying 150 tonnes of cotton, enough to make a goodly sum right under the noses of the customs men. I had a chance to break free from Unsworth, to no longer be financially beholden to him, and the plan might have worked, were it not for Heathcliff.

After-sight is a terrible torment, as is the blindness that arises from pridefulness, for initially I found him a very valuable charge, worthy of all my efforts to secure him.

These efforts were again on hold during those weeks, or they seemed to be, for I knew Carter had him in hand. I sometimes wondered what new ordeal Heathcliff was suffering, but I consoled myself that the boy would not refuse to leave with me a second time. Perhaps some of it was beneath me, but Heathcliff would not be Heathcliff, were it not for the indignities heaped upon him in the Tower.

When I returned to the gaol nearly three weeks after seemingly abandoning Heathcliff, the warden met me at the gate.

'I'm glad you heeded my advice,' I said, alluding to the clean courtyard.

Carter laughed, nervously I thought, and led me to a room that served as his office.

It was a stark chamber, with only a small desk, four trays filled with browned paper and two chairs. He motioned for me to sit in one chair, whilst Carter scraped the other on the stone flags and tried to settle comfortably in it. The room was painted white, but damp bloomed like dianthus on the walls.

'This is very formal,' I said, indicating the desk that divided us like a border between two countries. 'Are you about to reveal the boy is dead?'

Carter smiled uneasily. I would reclaim my money, every shilling, if he had lost my charge.

'No', Carter said slowly. 'He is not dead.'

'So, what is he, if not dead?' I asked, and when Carter did not immediately reply, I added, 'Come now, don't trifle with me. You know I'm not to be sported with.'

'Yes, of course, Mr Morgan. I didn't think that for a moment. It's merely that the boy has made quite an impression on the other gaolers…'

'Do not dally with me,' I snapped. 'What is the boy's situation?'

'I did everything you asked of me,' he said, before pausing and peering over my head towards the open door. 'You can see for yourself now. I sent for the boy when I received word that you were calling this afternoon.'

Heathcliff was being led across the courtyard by two gaolers, and if Carter had not informed me of his identity, I would never have taken the wretched thing for the boy who nearly knocked down Ben Naylor. Heathcliff appeared older, with hunched shoulders and a complexion as lined as an autumn leaf. If I were made of softer stuff, I would have pitied him, but instead I knew I could use this to admonish the warden.

'He is hardly the same boy,' I said to Carter.

'You wanted him brutalised, Mr Morgan, and my guards acquiesced.'

'Brutalised not enfeebled,' I said, glaring at him. 'If you've rendered him useless, I will petition Mr Unsworth to install a new warden.'

His face became as pale as the wall behind him, but he beckoned the gaolers forward with an air of composure.

'He is not useless, as you will see,' he said. 'It looks worse than it is, I assure you.'

I followed Heathcliff's slow advance. His legs seemed as good as wasted and the upper body that withstood Ben Naylor three weeks before, was now shrunken and stooped like a beggar's. His hair had been shaved with such vigour that the cuts on his scalp still wept. He had been beaten frequently, and before the injuries from the previous beating had time to heal. But within that debased frame there was still a scantling of strength remaining, for his eyes were pools of black fire.

'How is it with you, boy?' I asked, standing to face him.

When Heathcliff did not answer, I motioned for the gaolers to release him. He stumbled but remained standing; his legs trembled at the effort of it.

'Walk that way. Make use of your legs,' I commanded, wanting to take the measure of him. If Heathcliff had been genuinely broken, I would have abandoned him to his fate.

Heathcliff contracted his lips and took four slow steps into the room.

'Walk towards me, let me look at you,' I said.

Heathcliff turned and stood within two feet of me.

'What is your name?' I asked.

He mumbled a word that I did not catch. 'What did you say?'

'Heathcliff,' he said, more clearly. 'My name is Heathcliff.'

'And what is your family name?'

He seemed to consider for a moment, his eyes moving from side to side like a cornered animal.

'I don't have a family name.'

'Then what was the name of your master?'

'Earnshaw, but he was not my master.'

Earnshaw. The name was familiar to me.

'Are you sure of that name?' I asked, with a degree of wonder, for if it was the Earnshaw I knew, it changed matters. But then I considered how many Earnshaws there were in the world, and how I had not heard of Unsworth's associate for many years.

'It is no matter,' I said, before he could respond. 'Are you ready to leave this place, Heathcliff?'

The boy's gaze fell on Carter, still sitting uncomfortably behind his desk.

'Aye,' he said, turning his eyes to me. 'I am.'

Ben Naylor was usually at the helm of the wagon, but I didn't think it was wise on this occasion: I didn't want Heathcliff to associate me with the man who knocked him down, not yet. So, it was one of Unsworth's men that waited outside the Tower. Heathcliff reeked and looked the vagabond, with his shaven head and bruises, but the driver wisely did not note the state of my travelling companion. Heathcliff perched stiffly on the seat opposite, not from a sense of anticipation but from discomfort it seemed to me, and would not look at me.

'I'll engage the services of a doctor this afternoon,' I said. 'He'll see you right.'

He remained silent as we travelled between the grey bricks of Water Street, but as the Exchange, in all its columns and pomp, rose from behind the buildings, Heathcliff lifted his head to get a clearer view of the stone heads, of the absurd dome. He would look, then lower his eyes, as though determined to feign indifference.

But then, wincing, he stretched his legs, made himself more comfortable and regarded me with a hint of interest in place of the hatred that I had become accustomed to. It was the first step in claiming him as my own, or so I thought then.

'What are the statues on that building?' he asked, in that wild accent of his. It summoned barren landscapes in a harsh country, far away.

'They're symbols of commerce,' I said, and when Heathcliff looked at me blankly, I added, 'Symbols of trade, of buying and selling. Some of the sculptures are to do with the sea, but there are also bales of cotton – to reveal our links to that trade. This is a mighty city, Heathcliff. A prosperous city.' It was too early to discuss my business with Heathcliff, but I thought it would not hinder him to know some details of the world he would soon inhabit.

We slowed down as we emerged from under the shadow of the Exchange onto Castle Street. Heathcliff's attention moved furtively from one scene to another, and I realised this was his first view of Liverpool, and what a sight it must be. I envied him, for I saw only the narrowness of the ill-built road and the mean, dirty streets. He looked upon these imperfections with a wonderment he could not conceal. He was unperturbed by the reek of the Old Shambles, which protruded warm, fly-filled meat onto a street that was stained brown with blood. Perhaps his experiences in the Tower had deadened his senses. He stared at the rabble of traders and buyers, grand ladies and fishwives, butchers and hoteliers, until he seemed to forget the pain in his legs.

I did not suspect then that Heathcliff was kin to this city, to those alleys, that he was born on the very streets he now gawped at, and that his plight became Abe Earnshaw's lot. Heathcliff said, much later, that he recalled some details of his early childhood: of the narrow streets, of a kindly tanner with rough hands who gave him a coal shed to sleep in, and a lady who sometimes brought him cold meats wrapped in greased brown paper and spoke to him in words that were now strange to him. This was a home-coming for Heathcliff, and his return seemed to strip away his sullenness to reveal a boy who was interested and perhaps, I wondered then, not without intelligence.

We passed the Corn Market and picked up speed as the road widened into Pool Lane. The church of St George stood over us, and Heathcliff's eyes narrowed at its distinctness. He gazed long at the pillory, empty for once but with the scraps of recent prisoners: pressed cabbages, spatters of horse manure and rocks, an abundance of rocks. I imagined the congregation from St George descending the steps, heavy with the stones they would throw at the sinned and the sinful. I imagined their lightness of foot as they turned away, their pockets empty.

'Never trust God-fearing men, Heathcliff,' I said. 'The fuckers will damn you to save themselves.'

'Aye,' he replied, meeting my eyes. 'I know all about them folk.' His face darkened as he seemed to remember past injuries. 'They named me devil, told me to read my Bible and be good. I threw that accursed book into the flames.'

It was the first time he had offered anything of his previous life, and it confirmed, in my mind at least, that I could make something noteworthy of him. His meagre blasphemy was derisory, but he reminded me of myself at his age – at war with the world and wilfully far from home.

As we moved south from St George's and emerged into the open, we fell silent once more, for to view the Old Dock from Pool Lane is to truly behold Liverpool for the first time, to see her beating heart and understand the workings of her: her passions and caprices, her darkness and potential. Every man has a master, whether he realises it or not. I thought Heathcliff would find his at the dock, just as I had before him; but Liverpool was not to be his mistress, and I was not his master for long.

Yet at that time, and for some time afterwards, the Old Dock, and the sails which swelled and stirred restlessly in the breeze from the Mersey, held Heathcliff in thrall.

'How are they here, in the middle of all these buildings?' he said, noticing the bowsprits that extended over the quayside, the taut ropes, and the breasts of the comely figureheads. 'I could almost touch them.'

It was at this point, as the driver negotiated the wagon between the barrels piled high along the dock and the customs men waiting to weigh and value, that Heathcliff, despite the humiliations I had bestowed upon him, revealed his nature to me.

He sat squarely and did not take his eyes away from mine as he spoke. 'There's a fortune to be made here and I've a mind to partake in it.'

'Then you'll have to do as you're told. Can you do that?'

He regarded me for a moment and then smiled. 'Aye,' he said. 'I can.'

So, when we arrived at my dwelling, Madoc House, situated on the south side of the dock, pressed between a rope maker and an ironmonger, Heathcliff did not blanch at the sight of

Ben Naylor waiting at the door or fly at him when he grinned and said, 'So, my little black bastard, you're not dead.'

Heathcliff skulked around the upper floors for days. He confined himself to the attic: a dreary, damp, cheerless place, but superior to his lodgings in the Tower. I would visit him up there, to coax him downstairs to more comfortable accommodation, but I'd always find him at the window, high above the dock, watching the loading and unloading of ships, the customs men measuring and counting, the dull-ship hands playing skittles with old cannon balls on the quayside, and he would not come down from his eyrie.

Ben Naylor's dislike was clear from the very beginning. He could hear the floorboards groan whenever Heathcliff moved, so he was always aware of his presence, even though he had not set eyes on him for days. He complained about the boy freely and consistently. I endured this for a time, but I soon grew tired of it. I did not, then, suspect the slow workings of revenge within Heathcliff, and I now see that Ben Naylor, for all his faults, had the measure of the boy.

When Heathcliff appeared five days later, I assumed it was hunger that brought him down, like a fledgling that's given up its parents for dead. He looked the vagabond more than ever, but he was sturdier on his feet, and he walked purposefully down the stairs.

'There's a tailor on the east side of the dock,' he said. 'If you want me to serve you, make me presentable.'

'*If you want me to serve you*,' Ben Naylor said, imitating the boy's accent.

He had installed himself on a stool near the fireplace in the hall. The embers were dying and as Heathcliff descended the final steps, Naylor removed one of his mud and shit-cladded boots and threw it at the boy. The boot struck Heathcliff on the side of the head, knocking him over.

'Get down here boy and get the fire going.'

Heathcliff got up and wiped the muck from his face.

'Nay, I will not,' he spat, clenching his fists. 'I'm not your slave, whoreson.'

'You little bastard. You do as I say, or I'll have you back in the Tower.'

Naylor was about to remove his other boot when I stepped in.

'Ben,' I said, lengthening the vowel in warning. 'Fetch your boot and clean all that shit from the staircase.'

Naylor stood, dismayed.

'This is a mistake, Ned,' Naylor said, his dislike for Heathcliff curdling into jealousy. 'The moment your back is turned, he'll...'

'Enough,' I said, raising my hand. 'You will learn to suffer his presence, Ben.'

Heathcliff uncurled his fists and watched Ben Naylor with interest.

'He's a stranger and a foreigner,' Naylor said, his eyes boring into me. 'He will murder us in our beds the moment our guard is down.'

'He has been here for five days, and yet we are still living,' I said. 'I'm growing impatient, Ben. I value your loyalty, but I'm fucking tired of hearing your complaints. You *will* suffer his presence, and you'll do it with a degree of restraint. Do you understand?'

Naylor's jaw tightened and his eyes emptied.

'Very well,' he said in a low voice.

Heathcliff picked up the boot and presented it to Naylor as though it were a gift.

Naylor snatched it from his hand and for a moment I thought he would hit him with it, but he seemed to think better of it and merely returned it to its original function as a shoe. He did not bow or take his leave or glance at Heathcliff. He did not clean the shit from the staircase. Instead, he strode from my presence and closed the outer door firmly behind him.

'Ben will come round,' I said to Heathcliff, once I knew for certain Naylor had gone.

'I have no quarrel with him,' Heathcliff said, shrugging his shoulders.

'Come,' I said, beckoning him, taking his claimed indifference to Naylor at face value. 'Let us forget Ben for the moment. Show me that tailor you spoke of.'

Heathcliff became my ward, my shadow, my spy.

At first, he merely ran errands for me – small at first, such as fetching packages of sterling or contraband from the smaller docks. He was given an education in those weeks: he came to know my ship-builder contacts at the Salthouse and my tobacco associates at King's. He was thorough in his work and eager to learn, so my vanity was appeased, and I began to trust in both his regard for me and in his loyalty to my enterprises.

He was a wilful, wild thing, and I was flattered that I, and I alone, had seemingly tamed him. He was docile, even in Ben Naylor's presence, so I did not fear him and had no reason to suspect that the ferocity I had seen on our first meeting was merely lying dormant within him, biding its time. He was of use to me, and I admit that his usefulness blinded me to his true nature.

I came to depend on his presence during meetings. He would watch my associates from his stool in the corner near the hearth and would alert me afterwards to any unevenness or suspected betrayal. He rarely spoke in company, for I think he had become sensible of his speech and mode of address. My associates were a rough knot of ne'er-be-goods, but many had prominent positions with the most prosperous merchants in Liverpool, so their speech needed to beguile their true selves; they had learnt to speak clearly, gracefully and with softened accent.

Heathcliff listened intently and wrote in the notebook he had taken to carrying about his person. It was bound in brown leather, and he had ingrained a silvery H on the cover in lead. I was not sure where he had acquired it, but these books are commonplace on the dock. Merchants use them for recording their haul, and the customs men write lists of ships and cargo in them. I suppose he might have stolen it or taken a share of the sterling he often took delivery of and purchased it from the stationer on Pool Lane. I *was* concerned when this notebook appeared, and I insisted on checking it often. It seemed to contain merely notes from meetings written in tight, black scrawl, like rows of spiders on the page. I stressed the importance of keeping the notebook safe, since I did not want the particulars of my business in the wrong hands, but he was an apt pupil and I contented myself that apt pupils make notes.

When I asked how he learnt his letters, he became morose, like the 'other' Heathcliff, the boy with black fire within him. It seemed a clergyman taught him, and when his tutor was sent away, a sister or a friend, I did not understand his exact relationship to her, continued his education. He could not bear further questioning and would not reveal the female's name. He was no simple runaway, that much was clear.

His notebook was open on his lap when I called a meeting a few weeks before the planned piracy of Unsworth's ship, the *Isabella*. After the carelessness of the previous affair, I was eager to appease Unsworth by seeming to manage the next more efficiently. None of us were paid after the *Fortune* misadventure – a point that irked me. The other men involved in the enterprise were also maddened by Unsworth's pecuniary chastisement. It is bad management to deny your workers the one thing that secures their loyalty.

Thomas Duke was the first to voice his discontent.

'Who's to say, Ned, that we will gain anything from this? Unsworth is a damned niggard: dry-fisted and as crooked as a ship in a storm,' he leaned forward, warming to his subject. 'The last calamity was not our doing; no man could have thwarted it. We deserve recompense for the risks we took so freely.'

The other three men assembled in my parlour nodded their heads at Duke's words.

'Unsworth acted unfairly, but he is necessary for all our

fortunes in this town,' I responded, looking directly at Thomas Duke, whilst also testing the loyalty of the others. 'He uses his own contacts to protect us and without him, we would be hawkers, dealing in petty goods, living in outhouses behind the taverns of Gibraltar Street.'

'Yes, Ned,' Thomas said, smiling. 'We all know *you* are Unsworth's man, but,' he said, looking at the others, 'I say we want no share in this enterprise.'

Samuel Abbot nodded, but the other two men, John Brown, and George Wright, turned away from Thomas.

'John and I are willing to give you, and Unsworth, another chance,' George said.

Thomas shook his head and stood up, scraping his chair against the flagstones: a sound I detest.

'You're fools,' he began. 'Unsworth is not to be trusted and, by association, neither is Ned. We put ourselves in great risk for him, for both of them, and there is no recompense, no reward for our efforts.'

'I'm sorry you feel that way, Thomas,' I said, leaning back in my chair. 'We have worked together for many a year and not without profit. Unsworth is like all grand men, he has his own caprices and rages, but do not doubt that he is the most powerful man in Liverpool. He has more black cargo than any other, he owns the largest plantations and perhaps he does not share his wealth as freely as he might.' I shrugged and held up my hands to signify that I also had not benefitted in recent months from Unsworth's riches. 'But I do have a plan, if you will hear it, Thomas.'

Thomas surveyed the room and walked heavily towards the hearth. He rested his arm on the mantlepiece, attempting to be the master of the situation, which chafed me.

'The more I consider it, perhaps this venture isn't for you after all,' I said coldly, standing to face him. 'I think you have forgotten yourself this evening, Thomas.'

I found Heathcliff within the darkness and inclined my head to him. 'Heathcliff, escort Mr Duke out.'

Thomas started when he knew there was another person in the room but seemed to relax when he realised it was not Ben Naylor.

'Who is this? Fraternising with lascars now, Ned?' he asked, his upper lip curling slightly.

When I first knew the boy, he would have flared at this insult, but the new Heathcliff merely glared at Thomas Duke and left it at that.

'He is my ward, and no lascar.'

Thomas was visibly curious, but I would not elaborate.

A smothering silence grew whilst he squinted at every corner, trying to see through the darkness, and then asked, nervously, 'Where is Ben Naylor?'

'Ben is in the hall and will make sure you get back to Rodney Street in one form, or other.'

Thomas wavered and hovered for a moment before deciding to sit, lightly, in the chair he had a moment ago pushed aside.

I had very little time for him. He was a querulous bastard and if I could do without him, I would. But he had some useful lads, handy with their fists and able to hold their nerve, so Thomas had to be appeased, and threatened, when necessary, for despite his boldness I believed that in truth he was a coward.

Heathcliff settled back into his corner and continued to mark my guests. His presence troubled them, for they grew quiet and watchful, their eyes shifting from me to my 'mysterious ward', who sat silently and still behind me.

In time, George, growing impatient with the delay and wanting to relieve the ill-feeling, addressed me.

'What is this plan you spoke of, Ned?'

I made myself comfortable in my chair, rearranging the cushion, attempting to convey the appearance of patience and ease. In truth, I wanted Ben Naylor to pummel Thomas Duke's head against the hearth-stone. One word and it would be done. This certainty composed me, and I was able to continue dispassionately.

'Thomas is right. I have, in recent times, been so closely allayed with Mr Unsworth, that I have become *his man*, so to speak.' I waited for Thomas' surprise to settle, before continuing. 'But his unbending will has left all of us poorer.'

The men nodded and I knew I was on secure ground.

'By consequence, I propose that when we are in possession of the goods, in this case, nearly 150 tonnes of cotton, that we take a much bigger cut of the profit than we are accustomed to.'

'Ned,' George interrupted. 'Unsworth knows the value of his cargo: 150 tonnes – that's five thousand pounds at least. We will be discovered, and then what?'

I leaned back in my chair and smiled. They considered me a half-wit.

'I have been in communication with the captain of the *Isabella* – a sharp fellow by the name of Cox. I met with him before his voyage to the African coast, some twelve months hence. I received *this* letter,' I produced the article in question, 'eight weeks ago, from Captain Cox, the day before he planned to sail back across the Atlantic with his shipment.'

I opened the letter and read it aloud.

Mr Morgan,

All is set for our departure early tomorrow morn. The weather is favourable – clear with moderate wind, thus I do not anticipate a problematic crossing.

Expect the Isabella *between the morning of November 3rd and the evening of November 6th. I would suggest posting a watch in West Kirby, with an eye on the Irish sea.*

If, upon the receipt of this letter, my seal is damaged, then we are undone, and I pray that Mr Unsworth is merciful.

> *I remain yours,*
> *William Cox*

The men gazed at me in wonder.

'Some of us will be positioned in Formby, as planned, and as Unsworth expects,' I began to explain, 'but the ship will be stranded in Crosby, where the rest of us will amass. The chief pilot for that evening is a young man named Campbell. Ben Naylor will see to him. Unsworth will have no choice but to believe the evidence before him: that Cox lost control of the ship; that the sea retreated and much of the cargo was taken by expeditious pirates,' I paused briefly, and with a smile, added, 'It's common knowledge that the coast is brimming with these reprobates.'

The men snorted at the irony, but Thomas Duke would not be soothed. 'You spoke of how we need Unsworth, his protection,' he said. 'So why would you suggest that we act against him?'

'Unsworth has been good to me. Very good,' I said, the room quiet once more. 'Until the *Fortune* misadventure, he had contributed massively to my fortune. I was able to purchase Madoc House. But my reputation is my own, separate from my benefactor.' I leaned back in my chair so that I could look each man in the eye. 'Many of my contacts are my own, hard-forged. Despite my relative independence, I still want to maintain my alliance with Unsworth – *our* alliance with him. He is not a man I want working against us. So, when this emprise is completed, he will not put the blame on us. I will make sure of that.'

'How will you make sure of it?' Samuel Abbot asked. 'How do you know Cox won't reveal all when he is pressed?'

'The dead cannot speak, Samuel.'

There was silence.

'No,' Samuel eventually said, grinning. 'They cannot.'

'Once we are in possession of the cargo,' I continued, 'my contact at the Salthouse Dock will store it in one of his warehouses, until it is safe to transfer it on the canal. I have a buyer in Manchester, prepared to pay handsomely for it.'

The room fell stone-still as the men considered my plan.

'Shall I give you a moment to discuss my proposal?' I asked, moving to get up.

'As long as *he* leaves with you,' Thomas Duke said, pointing to where Heathcliff was positioned.

I looked to where the boy was partially concealed in the corner and realised, they would be ignorant of his presence if I had not betrayed it earlier.

'Ah, I must insist that he stays in the room,' I said.

Thomas Duke's eyes narrowed. 'Ben Naylor isn't even permitted to be privy to our meetings. Why is this boy given the privilege?'

I latticed my fingers together and remained silent.

Thomas persisted. 'I don't like the look of him, Ned. Can he be trusted with an affair as perilous as this one?'

'What offends you, Thomas?' I asked, stepping closer to him, keeping my chin raised. 'His youth? His strangeness? Or is it his complexion? I find his swarthiness becoming, for he can hide in dark places and go unnoticed.'

'Ah, so he is your spy?'

'He is many things,' I said, sensing it was not the time to announce him as my successor; a plan I had barely articulated, even to myself.

'But his strangeness is of a particular kind, for he is a foreigner *and* a stranger.'

'I was a stranger once, Thomas, and as a lad, foreign to this town.'

'Wales is not even half a day's ride from here,' Thomas said, grinning. 'There are more Welsh and Irish in Liverpool than Lancashire men.'

There was a pause whilst I considered how best to proceed. 'He is learning the business,' I conceded. 'Therefore, the boy must stay.'

Thomas looked beyond me and searched for Heathcliff in the corner.

'Does he not speak? Is he mute?'

'No, he knows when to talk and when to remain silent – invaluable in a servant, do you not think?'

Thomas Duke sighed and shrugged his grievance away, turning his chair so that Heathcliff could only see him from behind.

Heathcliff informed me later that all the men followed Thomas Duke's example when I'd left the room, and murmured to each other under their breaths, so that Heathcliff could only hear fragments of conversation.

All the chairs were facing the right way when I returned and were evenly spaced out, as though I had walked into my own trial.

But when the men departed Madoc House that evening, they left having swallowed their scruples and with a pledge to enact my plan.

Thomas and his men would amass at Formby, a safe distance from Crosby – for I did not entirely trust him. George, Samuel, and my men would muster on Crosby Sands. Cox would arrive between November 3rd and November 6th. I had connections in West Kirby, on the Wirral peninsula, who would send word when the *Isabella* reached the North Wales coastline.

All was precise, or as precise as is possible when ships are assailable to storms and piracy and mutiny. Cox seemed an unerring man, and he did prove true, which soothed me in the days after Heathcliff's betrayal. It served as proof that I was not typically so short-sighted in my judgement.

Heathcliff was present throughout most of my dealings. He became a regular face in Unsworth's townhouse, but I had no reason to suspect conspiracy. Only Ben Naylor perceived that the threat would not hail from the seas.

'What does the boy write in that notebook?' he asked me, for what must have been the fourth or fifth time.

'I check that notebook after every meeting,' I said. 'And as I have already explained countless fucking times, he is keeping a record of the meeting for me to peruse afterwards. Why is this so difficult to understand, Ben?'

'Watch him,' he said, shaking his head. 'If something goes awry with him then one word from you and the bastard will find himself sunk in a dock.'

'If he is somehow deceiving me,' I said, laying a hand on Ben's shoulder, 'I'll put him in the dock myself.'

But, of course, it was not *what* he was writing that was significant, and I was a fool not to see it.

After receiving word from my contact in West Kirby, we moved to assemble on Crosby Sands on the evening of November 5th.

We departed Liverpool in the late afternoon, riding in separate groups up the coastline, guided by a line of blue bonfires and the smell of damp wood burning. In nearly every village there were effigies, some already blackened from being placed too near the flames, others crudely carried by children squabbling over pennies. The villages spilled onto the marshes, where broods of urchins spent their days searching for the dregs of shipwrecks or the leavings of weak-kneed pirates fleeing from the revenue men. Their pickings were sold to dealers in Liverpool. The oriental china, silks and opium pipes were never exhibited in the shop windows, for fear of the customs men. But there were back rooms and basements, and scores of merchants were known to deal in contraband. I acquired branding irons and chains from one such merchant on Mersey Street. The children found more than just porcelain and pipes in the mire.

I rode with Heathcliff and two others – Samuel Abbot's men. Heathcliff rode next to me, cock-sure on his reclaimed colt, the bonfires from the coastline setting his eyes aflame.

We were making good time when Heathcliff suddenly halted his horse.

'What is it?' I asked, looking back along the road. 'Are we being followed?'

'I want to burn something,' he said, pointing to the coastline. 'In one of those fires.'

My associates, both sensible men, stared at Heathcliff with wide eyes.

'What the fuck is wrong with him?' one of them asked, speaking directly to me. 'We don't have time for this.'

'Go without me,' Heathcliff said. 'I will be directly behind you.'

'Just leave him, Ned,' the other man said.

'I will not go without him,' I said. 'You know Unsworth's grain; he will end all of us if we are caught tonight. I want everyone in their allotted place.'

Samuel's men waited expectantly, their eyes set on the darkening sky.

'Go ahead to Crosby,' I said to them. 'Tell Ben Naylor I will be there directly.'

The men paused for a moment and were, I think, on the verge of refusing to go without me. But sense overcame their instinct: they would rather be sheltered in the dunes of Crosby sands than out in the open in the half-light, and so they turned and rode into the fast-approaching night.

When they were out of sight, I confronted Heathcliff.

'What is this?' I asked. 'Are you suddenly fearful?' When Heathcliff didn't respond, I asked, half laughingly, 'Or do you mean to betray me?'

'You saved me from the Tower,' he said. 'How could I betray you when you've done so much for me?'

His tone was not to my liking.

'Do you *dare* sport with me, boy?'

'No,' he answered, looking me directly in the eyes. 'I'll be moments, and then we can be on our way.'

Heathcliff broke eye contact and dismounted his colt before I could protest. He strode through the marsh, his boots sinking an inch into the mud, towards the nearest driftwood bonfire. I cursed him and reflected on how Ben Naylor would have stayed on his horse.

I wondered if Heathcliff was nervous about the evening's enterprise. Why else would he delay? As I watched his deliberately slow movement through the mire, suspicion grew within me. Had Ben been right all along about him?

I could have left him there and taken his horse with me, but as I watched him slowly make his way to the bonfire, I still saw myself in him, on the day of my first undertaking for Unsworth. I shat myself and would have bolted if Unsworth had not taken me in hand, and so I shook off my suspicions.

I was a damned fool.

I watched as Heathcliff took the pencil and notebook from his coat pocket. I was accustomed to this behaviour and so didn't find it strange; he carried his writing utensils with him habitually. He was so focused on his writing that he did not at first observe the mud-children gathering around him, until they closed in on him with their grabbing, straining hands. The girl carrying the guy dropped the rough effigy and joined her fellows in engirdling Heathcliff. When he stood tall and lunged at them, they backed away, but it was merely a game to them, and they drew nearer the moment Heathcliff was still. I found this scene unsettling, uncanny even.

'Heathcliff!' I called. 'We must leave now. Stop this business and get back on your horse!'

He turned to glare at me, and then, seemingly without the use of his eyes, he reached for one of the children – the girl that had carried the effigy – and held her against him, his arm around her neck. He lifted her and squeezed. The girl, in some panic, screamed and kicked the air. Heathcliff's actions had, what I assumed, the desired effect – the other children withdrew to a safer place. After a few moments, Heathcliff dropped the girl. She collapsed at his feet, clutching her throat, gasping. He kicked her away and she half-ran half-stumbled after her companions. The beggar-children dispersed, leaving the guy face down in the mud.

Heathcliff had kept his eyes on me throughout this queer

affair, and I was discomposed, for the landscape was not to my taste. The light was fading, the distant sea was silent, and each of those dreadful bonfires cast an eerie, flickering likeness on the marsh. I turned briefly from Heathcliff's scrutiny and watched the last of the day fading into what I hoped would be a moonless night.

When my attention returned to Heathcliff, he was at the base of the bonfire, kneeling and writing in his notebook. He ripped a page, folded it, and threw it into the fire. He stood there for too long, watching the paper burn and ascend in golden-blue sparks.

I had no understanding of this ritual, but it recalled the strange stories told on the docks. I often jeered at these tales and directed the sailors who transmitted them to the nearest church, where they would find superstition enough, but I felt differently on that evening. It may have been the dimming light, or my nervousness and need to reach Crosby, but Heathcliff's actions brought to mind the tales of sailors returned from the colonies. They spoke of strange things, things not readily explained by Englishmen. They feared the savages, who would chant and wail in the ship's hold, unsettling the crew and the sea beneath them. They claimed these practices could send sailors mad and sink ships. Did Heathcliff emerge, half-formed and cursing, from such a ship?

Heathcliff was ignorant of his origins – of that I was certain. I wondered if he was fashioning a history for himself in his notebook, in his nearly incomprehensible, childish hand. Which part of his imagined history did I see him burn? Or was it his future he had sent up to the sky?

Afterwards, we did not speak of the bonfires, the children, or his strange conduct, as we rode on the flat, endless road to Crosby. We rode in silence, with the sun setting behind us, removing the paltry warmth from the day. I rode with one hand on the bridle and the other fastening my coat around my neck.

'How much farther?' Heathcliff asked over the sound of hooves on stone.

'Half an hour,' I answered. 'Damn you, we were meant to be there before nightfall.'

We rode against time, against the fast-gathering darkness, and against my own instinct, for I feared some ill-luck, but superstition is the sanctuary of the weak-minded. I would not hide within it like a whey-blooded child.

Beneath the descending line of light, the outline of Crosby's sand-downs appeared. I pulled the reigns and slowed to almost a standstill. Heathcliff did the same. I tried to listen beyond the waves and the rustling of birds and rodents in the thickets bordering the road. When I was certain there were no unusual sounds, I rode nearer to the downs and gave the signal: a low whistle. Instead of a reply, Ben Naylor's giant shape appeared, just as the last of the sun set behind us, wax-red and bleeding.

'Where have you been?' he asked. 'The others are fear-struck. I had to leave them for I was tempted to beat them silent.'

I looked at Heathcliff, who dismounted his colt and moved towards us.

'Heathcliff had some business with the bonfires,' I said.

'Business with the bonfires?' Ben repeated.

'It is of no importance,' I said, focusing on the task at hand. 'Take us to the other men, and quickly.'

'I'll see to the horses first,' Heathcliff cut in. 'They need to be well-hidden.'

He was right, the horses would need to be out of sight, but I hesitated before agreeing, for after his behaviour on the road, I wanted to keep him close. But I could not reveal this to Ben Naylor; his dislike of the boy was such that any misgivings on my behalf would be a victory for him. He would water that doubt until it grew into certainty.

'Very well,' I said eventually. 'But hurry to the beach once the horses are safely stored.'

Heathcliff nodded and led the horses across the road and towards a thicket in the near distance.

'What was he doing with the bonfires?' Ben Naylor asked again.

'It was a whim and of no consequence,' I said. 'Come, take me to the others.'

'They're a little further this way,' Ben said, leading me over the dunes. 'They have the boats ready, buried under seaweed, ropes and tarpaulin.'

When we arrived at the meeting point, the men were waiting in the shadows, and they were indeed uneasy, as Ben had described. Two of the men, George Wright and another, flew up the beach to speak with me.

'Where have you been?' George asked, using his arms to gesticulate his distress. 'We would have left, if you hadn't set your dog to guard us,' he said, pointing to Ben Naylor.

'I take offence at that,' Ben said.

'You have my apologies, George,' I said. 'We were held up on the road.'

'Where is the lascar?' he asked. 'Is he out of favour?'

'He is hiding the horses,' I said. 'Where is the boat?'

'Over yonder,' the other man answered, pointing to the seafront. 'She's ready to go.'

I now recognised him as Richard Withers, a discreet and trustworthy fellow.

'Richard,' I said, shaking his hand.

I glanced behind me and there was still no sign of Heathcliff.

'Ben,' I said, 'go and check on Heathcliff. Hurry him along.'

Ben Naylor sighed but did as he was told and hurried back towards the sand dunes.

I looked to the coastline, but my eyes did not immediately adjust to the darkness, despite the brightness of the stars, so I had to search deeply for the vessel Richard was referring to. When I did see it, I wondered how I could have missed it. The tarpaulin had been removed and the outline of men was visible, moving rapidly around the boat. It was a cutter, like the boats used by the customs men to intercept smugglers. Someone lit a lamp and it hung faintly on its prow.

'Is that the cutter you seized, Richard?' I asked, for I admired acts of piracy, especially when it was against the crown.

'That's the one,' he answered, his eyes glinting.

I was about to ask another question, when there was a whistle from one of the men near the cutter. I looked to the horizon, and the *Isabella* emerged out of the darkness like a mythical sea-dragon, its sails like great black wings. Two lamps were lit, and like eyes, they blinked their cypher to those of us waiting on land.

I ran down to the cutter, pushed a man aside and used the end of an oar to block out the light and send a message to Captain Cox. *We are here.*

'Fetch me two more lamps!' I barked at the man nearby. I heard shuffling feet, and the lamps were presented to me.

'Light them,' I commanded, and when the man did not move, I looked for Ben Naylor and Heathcliff, but they were no-where in sight. There was a moment of unease at their absence, but the business at hand was more urgent.

'Move, man!' I shouted, shaking the man.

He fumbled with the casements and eventually both lamps were lit. The light illuminated his face: he was a boy, no older than twelve.

'Well done,' I said, softening my sounding.

The boy helped me to position the lamps so the ship could be steered precisely. Cox would lower the anchor half a mile from the shoreline, and although the ship was still over a mile away, she was moving at such speed that she would be upon us in no time at all.

I quickly gathered George and his men around me, who stood silently, awaiting instruction. I chose eight to remain on land to unload the goods, and I selected another eight to accompany me in the boat.

'Have you seen Ben Naylor?' I asked the men, as we began to heave the boat onto the shoreline. I needed him to take care of Cox if the need arose. The ship was so near now that I could hear the masts creaking in the breeze, but I was loath to depart without Ben by my side. I began to wonder if Heathcliff and Ben had argued and fought, it would explain both their absences – it would not be the first time and without me there to mediate, they could, if the urge took them, bludgeon each other to death. The more I thought of it, the more I became convinced. I cursed myself for sending Ben Naylor to fetch the boy.

'Wait,' I said, letting go of the boat. The others stopped pushing and turned to me. Their faces were illuminated by the moon and the flickering light of the lantern, and I could tell by their features, their set jaws and deep frown lines as they looked at one another, that their regard for me was ebbing.

'I will be a moment,' I said, aware simultaneously of the proximity of the ship, the men's impatience, and the possibility of seeing both Heathcliff and Ben Naylor spread out on the road. The boy was strong enough to get the better of Ben now, and despite the unsettling events on the way to Crosby, I was hopeful that if I had to part with one of them, then it would be Ben splayed on the road.

I ran up the beach towards the sand-dunes and road beyond, but before reaching the dunes, I stopped. Standing on the downs was a line of figures, dark except for the lamps they held, lighting their faces and their livery. Those not carrying lanterns held muskets, which were all pointing at me. I turned to find the other men, but most were in the cutter, attempting to escape by sea, and the others scurried like sand flies in all directions. Nobody had alerted Cox, so the *Isabella* creaked quietly, not far from the shore.

I placed my hands high, so the revenue men would know I was not armed. I expected them to shout, to run down and restrain me, to beat me perhaps, but they stood in a uniform line, gripping their lanterns and muskets, as though waiting. I had determined to call out, when two other figures appeared amongst them. I recognised the first as Heathcliff, his face livid in the blinking lamplight, and next to him, the tall figure of Unsworth, holding what I quickly understood to be Heathcliff's notebook.

Miss Henrietta Unsworth

Speke Hall and Liverpool
May – August 1782

Speke Hall – May 13th
My dear Charlotte,

I cannot express how splendid it was to have you back at Speke
– the house has been a shell since you decided to marry and
abandon me. It was very careless of you to be carried away by
John! I am certain he does not deserve you, and I told him so
on many occasions during your stay. Do not be vexed – I believe
he understands the turn of my humour and I am obliged
through sisterly affection to approve of his. We got on handsomely.

As I am sure you have conjectured from your visit, Speke holds
very little charm for me since you wed. The servants rattle in
empty rooms, closing the curtains that I open to let the light
in, whispering and watching all day: not through malevolence
I am certain, but through an infectious tedium. Thank goodness
I have Hana – she is the best of them. She sits with me in the
afternoons, in her bright headscarf, recounting exotic tales,
uttered in strange syllables, transporting me from the confines
of this prison-house. Oh, I know you must find me effusive!
And perhaps I am behaving theatrically, but it is isolation that
has made me thus.

Nobody comes here, Charlotte – nobody of any significance at
least; the post-boy calls every day, as does the grocer, and the
milk-seller. Papa's business keeps him in Liverpool and when
he does return, it is for a night at a time. He never brings
company with him – no entertainment or even the promise of
any pastime. Since your visit, I have only been riding once. I
read novels Papa would disapprove of, and I practise on the
pianoforte until my fingers are rigid. I walk in the gardens. I
paint frightful watercolours. I try to converse with the stable

boy, who appears embarrassed by my attentions. I do not wish to be irksome – it was not my intention when I began this letter, but I am so forlorn here in Speke. I think a change of setting would be beneficial, but Papa seems determined to keep me here.

This leads me to the purpose of this correspondence: to beg you to intervene on my behalf. Papa greatly esteems you and listens to your advice. If you could press upon him the state I am in, that I am reading the most scandalous books, producing ill-favoured art, and associating with stable-boys, I am sure he would allow me to remain with him in town this summer.

I await your reply.

Yours affectionately,
Henrietta

Hanover Street, Liverpool – May 25th
Dearest Charlotte,

You are an angel – I have long suspected thus. I will pluck a hundred swans in your honour. I will fashion you wings of such beauty that Daedalus would weep to behold them. You have delivered me, my angel, from that wretched house, from the gathering gloom that threatened to gnaw at my youth and happiness. I can only surmise what passed between you and Papa, but whichever arts you used to release me from Speke, I am grateful for them.

I have been installed in Hanover Street since Tuesday, and I am full of wonder. The house is a marvel – high ceilings, windows as tall as ships, and a white staircase that winds like clematis. Hana insists I have visited Hanover Street before, but I must have been very young, or my memory is failing. As for Liverpool, I think the town is very happily situated. Its inhabitants, although rough-hewn, are bursting with vitality. What a contrast to the lifelessness of Speke! I thought I would die there, Charlotte. I know you think me foolish, but one cannot keep a bird encaged and expect it to thrive.

I have only explored the environs of Hanover Street thus far. Papa has a map of the town on the wall of his room – Hana, when Papa is elsewhere, commits to memory the more interesting streets. As I professed in my previous letter, Hana is a marvel, and she is my guide. We walked the short distance to the Old Dock during our first outing, and I was very taken with it. The bustle, the wrangling, the concourse of a hundred different accents and languages – Liverpool is the world entire, but in miniature.

I am not permitted to roam from morning until evening as I would like since Papa is concerned about my safety. I am released during the afternoons to explore with Hana, therefore be assured, my dear Charlotte, I am in a much happier state than when I last wrote to you. Change is medicine for the soul, I am certain of it – the distractions of Liverpool have revived me.

There is one matter, however, that irritates me. I am afraid you will think me ungrateful. Even with a full understanding of our father's character, his actions seem excessive to me. Please do not be agitated or utter my grievances to Papa, for I do not wish to displease him. The particulars are these: when Hana and I venture from Hanover Street for our afternoon walk, Papa insists that we take one of his associates with us, to 'guarantee my safety', although I cannot discern any immediate threat to my person. If Papa had ever seen Hana in a temper, he would know that I do not need to be protected by a sullen, watchful boy barely older than I am.

Hanover Street is a busy, noisy townhouse with many comings and goings – the one constant seems to be the boy. Papa informed me of his name, but it was so unfamiliar and remote that I cannot recall it at all. I shall ask him on the next occasion he is sent to spy on me. He is a spy, Charlotte, I am certain of it. However, I will attempt to overcome my vexation, for there are amusements enough in Liverpool to divert me – even when accompanied by my swarthy shadow.

These amusements will, I am sure, excite you, my dear sister – can you stem your curiosity? I cannot supress my enthusiasm – I am near bursting! Oh, Charlotte, there is to be a grand ball to celebrate King George's recovery from his latest malady, and Papa has vowed to let me attend! You simply must be here for it. Do you think John could spare you for a week or two? Inform him that I am desolate without you, that you feel it to be your duty to accompany me to all social engagements, to keep me in check and prevent the degradation of our family name, and so forth. I am sure John can be convinced that my playfulness could easily descend into impropriety without you. I am content to play any part you see fit.

Do come, my dear Charlotte!

Yours affectionately,
Henrietta

Hanover Street, Liverpool – May 31st
My dearest Charlotte,

It grieves me that John is so unyielding – I long to have you here, sister! However, I understand that you are answerable to your husband, just as I am at the mercy of Papa's capriciousness. It is an affliction of our sex that we cannot be responsible for ourselves, do you not think? We never spoke of such things when we were both still at Speke. I suppose my youth must have rendered such matters immaterial, and Mama's illness and Papa's gradual removal from our presence made conversation about more worldly affairs seem inconsequential. There were more pressing concerns.

I am sorry you are unable to be with me. To preserve the appearance of playful agreeability, tell your husband that I am most displeased, that I will tax him greatly when I see him next. He *must* learn to fear my displeasure.

It grieves me to describe delights that you cannot partake in, I will thus attempt to check my elation at the prospect of a ball, even a ball of the magnitude that is currently planned. It will be a vast affair, as mentioned in my previous correspondence, to celebrate King George's recovery. There will be a constellation of guests from every respectable family in Liverpool, perhaps hundreds of people – more bodies than I have ever encountered. Perhaps John would alter his view if he knew the most illustrious personages in the land will attend the ball. I am certain it is worth mentioning this fact to him; there is nothing amiss in attending a gathering of respectable persons – to observe an event the whole world is celebrating. But I will not press you further, you are more than capable of persuasion when necessary.

The days since my previous letter have been filled with the purchasing of ribbons and lace. Papa has furnished me with a generous allowance, and I have very much enjoyed spending it in the shops of Castle Street. Hana and I spent much time deliberating the colour of my muslin, before fixing on a very light blue, to complement my eyes. My surly shadow grunted his protest and attempted to wait for us outside, but if he is to be my shadow then that is exactly what he shall be, thus I

dragged him inside and demanded his opinion on every article
I was presented with. When I shewed him the French lace, he
was finally so affronted that he uttered, 'My god, how your
father must wish he'd had sons!' and charged out of the shop. I
was excessively diverted! Hana disapproves of him — she utters
oaths under her breath when he is near, and she is very watchful
of him. I think him delightful. His name is Heathcliff — isn't
that capital? It brings to mind wild landscapes and unyielding
rock. He is dark-skinned in aspect, but he is not quite of Hana's
hue. His features are not unattractive. His eyes are black and
searching and they meet mine with a ferocity that is so
disarming that I blush and laugh, which seems to vex him
terribly. I am certain he will grow accustomed to my humour,
as everyone must. Hana certainly knows not to mind me.

Yours affectionately,

Your loving sister,
Henrietta

Hanover Street, Liverpool — June 6th
My dearest Charlotte,

I am excessively envious, dear sister, of your recent company.
They may have outstayed their welcome, but I wish very much
I could have been amongst the party — I would happily remain
until even the servants wished me gone! Surrey seems an
awfully long way from Hanover Street. I do hope Papa will
agree to let me visit soon. I long to see the house you describe
so warmly and, of course, I long to see you also. Are you certain
you cannot attend the ball? I would not be nearly as nervous
with you by my side. I make no apology for pestering you in
this matter, but if you ask me to desist then, of course, I shall.
I do not wish to be a bore!

In truth, despite your absence, Liverpool has revived me. The cobwebs of Speke have been blown away. Hanover Street's vast windows and high ceilings are so distant from the dark nooks of Speke that I can at last breathe. I do miss the gardens and the yews in the courtyard, for I could open my chamber window and touch the branches. I will mourn the berries this winter and the birds that make their home in the boughs, yet there are trees and parks aplenty in town. I am certain the attractions of Liverpool, its vigour, its shoals of people, will requite the loss of the yew trees this winter.

This brings me to my news. I am no longer Henrietta the Reader, or Henrietta the Tenacious, or even Henrietta the Nuisance; I am now Henrietta the Explorer! I had the most wonderful adventure yesterday – I am giddy with the memory of it! Hana has been indisposed the last few days and has taken to her bed. Papa is furious, although I cannot understand what it is to him. It is me that has suffered from her distemper – I have been trapped and shackled for days, viewing the world through windows. I am Prometheus, bound to have my liver eaten by a confounded eagle only for it to regenerate and for the ordeal to begin again. For three days, I remained perched at my window, until at last, I resolved to do what Prometheus could not – I determined to set myself free, to venture abroad without Hana. I know you will think me foolish, and with after-sight you are correct to think so, although it was a mighty adventure! Despite the happy outcome, I think it would be best if you do not mention the following to Papa. Rest assured, Charlotte, I am safe, but you know Papa's temperament.

I discovered, a few days before my excursion, the existence of a person named Doctor Graham, who recommends 'earth baths' as a cure for various complaints. I am not certain of his position as doctor, but he and his wife are currently encamped in a garden in the upper part of Fleet Street, buried up to their necks in earth. I heard it was quite a spectacle, therefore I resolved to view this diversion for myself. I felt no fear as I ventured forth. The dappled sunshine; the friendly glances from strangers; the warmth of a summer's day – all these impressions, coupled with my effervescence, led to a diminishing of my faculties. I did not perceive any danger, nor did I observe my shadow, Heathcliff, pursuing me at a distance.

I cannot account for his decision to pursue me. Perhaps he is of such a wicked nature that playing the spy befits him. Perhaps he has an infatuation. Perhaps he is merely performing his duty. If it the latter, then I should direct both my fire and my gratitude at another.

I arrived in Fleet Street by mid-morning when the street was filled with traders and patrons. Life bubbled and frothed around me, but I felt very separate – conspicuous despite taking pains to dress plainly and not draw attention to my person. However, the more I attempted to blend with the crowd, the more incongruous I became. On more than one occasion, I was approached by strangers who impertinently enquired my name, my residence, and my parentage. I explained to each that they would need to be formally introduced before I could reveal such information. One man, for I will not call him a gentleman, laughed and attempted to take hold of my arm. His teeth were like old piano keys. I was grateful when a younger, more presentable gentleman came to my aid.

He had such a happy disposition that I was entirely free with him. I explained that I was in search of Doctor Graham, and he offered to walk me to the gardens so that I would not come to harm. I kept a respectable distance from him, but he was so charming, and he looked so agreeable, that I informed him of my name. The effect was immediate. He repeated the name Unsworth and when I nodded, a strange smile spread across his face. He was utterly altered, just for a moment, then he was all charm and politeness once more. But I began to comprehend my foolishness and wished to be elsewhere. I made my excuses, but he said, 'My dear Miss Unsworth, I do not think you understand the situation,' and reached for my arm.

Just as my courage was about to desert me, Heathcliff appeared. I watched him emerge from the crowd, his coat bellowing, but he did not seem to see me. Instead, he took in his opponent's height, waist, and arms, and then, dear sister, the most surprising and thrilling thing happened: Heathcliff clutched the man by the throat, nearly lifting him off his feet. He pushed him against a wall, whilst the traders and patrons looked on. 'What is your name?' Heathcliff asked. He was squeezing the man's throat so tightly that he was unable to answer. Heathcliff whispered in the man's ear, I did not hear what was said, but the man's eyes bulged, and he shook his head most profusely. When Heathcliff finally released him, the rogue did not even glance at me – he picked up his hat and ran down a side street. The traders returned to their traffic. The entire incident was finished in less than a minute.

As you can imagine, my relief was instant, but my ease dissipated when Heathcliff turned to me. He had not yet assumed a presentable face. His eyes were lit coals, and for a moment, I feared he would strike me. I stepped back and attempted to assume a haughtiness that I did not feel equal to. 'What do you mean by this, Heathcliff?' I asked. 'How dare you pursue me in this manner? My father shall hear of it.'

Even as I uttered these words, I knew their vacuity. But their force seemed to remind Heathcliff of his position – he subdued the fire within him and returned his features to those of a sullen boy. 'Since you are here,' I said, continuing in the same vein, 'I would like you to escort me to the gardens so that I may observe Doctor Graham at his work.' Heathcliff smiled – I was amazed how it became him despite the pain it clearly took him to feign good-humour, and said, 'Come then, Miss Unsworth. I shall take you,' with no bow or lowering of his head. His manners are as rough as an uncut gem.

We did not engage in conversation until we arrived at the gardens, where he was so incensed by the scene before us, that he said to me, with disdain, I am sure of it – '*This* is why you ran away?' I explained that I had not 'run away', that I felt trapped in Hanover Street since Hana's illness, but he shook his head and said, with teeth bared, 'You know nowt about the world, or your father's place in it.' At the time, I did not mind his words – I was determined to find some enjoyment in the spectacle I had turned explorer to witness. Doctor Graham was, as I had heard, buried up to his neck in earth. Opposite him was his wife, who was also buried so that she faced him. This was very strange, but the most unorthodox feature of the performance, for that is what I believed it to be, was that they both wore powdered wigs and were florid with rouge. They did not converse but maintained eye contact constantly. I could not shake the thought that the heads were models of some sort, or more disturbingly, real but severed from their bodies. Heathcliff's displeasure seemed to fade after a minute or two and he began to brood on the heads, his right foot repeatedly kicking an embedded rock, in tedium I imagined. I found his weariness diverging and suggested that we remained. This proposal was not to his taste. He was determined to march me back to Hanover Street that instant, and what a miserable journey it was, Charlotte. There is little or no conversation to be had from him. I enquired of his family, and where he was born. I did all that was required of me, and yet I received no response. The only time I received any attention from him was when I asked how he learnt the art of strangulation. He said he would 'throttle' me if I uttered one more word – imagine that, Charlotte!

It seems, however, that we did reach an understanding. He intimated that he would not inform Papa of my exploits and I hinted that I would not tell Papa of his. It seems he is now my confederate, Charlotte, as are you. What fun!

Yours affectionately,
Henrietta

Hanover Street, Liverpool – June 10th
My dearest Charlotte,

I am gratified by your quick response to my letter dated June 6th but please do not concern yourself, dear sister – I am perfectly well and despite the flippant tone of my previous letter, I have no immediate plans to wander anywhere alone again.

Hana has roused herself and is ready to go out into the world again, and Heathcliff, despite your misgivings, is entrusted by Papa – I suppose he did come to my rescue rather heroically. It seems the 'gentleman' that addressed me with such impropriety had the appearance of respectability, but all the gallantry belongs to Heathcliff. I cannot fathom it myself, but there it is. I can only assume that Heathcliff's surprising violence and un-polished manners stem from a brutal childhood, which we cannot blame him for. He is a puzzle to me, but since that day in Fleet Street, he has barely acknowledged me. When I am out with Hana, he walks ten feet behind us and is ever watchful, so rest easy dear sister.

Now that the thrill of that strange day has faded somewhat, I have given the events some thought. Charlotte, do you know the nature of Papa's work? Is it respectable? Excuse my bluntness – I am beginning to see that I have no understanding of it. Heathcliff's words, about knowing nothing of the world or Papa's place in it, trouble me. What is Papa's position in the world? He seems universally liked and respected, but if that is true, why did that man react to strangely when I revealed my name? He *knew* me, Charlotte. If you have any intelligence concerning Papa's business, please relieve yourself of it in your next letter. Papa has no knowledge of my adventure, I am certain of it. Heathcliff has not made it public.

I do not enjoy this heaviness, but the ball will be a marvellous diversion – I am sure of it!

I apologise for the brevity of this letter – I wanted to respond quickly to allay your fears.

Your affectionate sister,
Henrietta

Hanover Street, Liverpool – June 15th
My dearest Charlotte,

Before I acquaint you with all the events of the last five days, I must first beg a few moments of your time to describe, in detail, the ball that held so much expectation. I have been a wretched fool, but I will come to that.

Do you remember the Exchange on Castle Street? I would not be surprised if you have forgotten it – there is nothing to recommend it. The building is so severe, so masculine: all Doric columns, iron, and hard lines. I do not envy Papa, who cleaves his time between the Exchange and the Customs House. When I discovered, a day or two ago, that it was to be the location of the ball, I believe I grimaced. Papa laughed heartily at my disgust and Heathcliff regarded me as though I were the most foolish thing in creation. When I lamented with Hana, she scolded me for caring for such things. With censure everywhere I turned, I resolved to make the most of it, and dressed as though I were attending a ball at a palace.

I wore blue muslin with the ribbons I mentioned in my previous letter. Hana fixed a bandeau in my hair – she would not permit me to wear powder, since I am 'only child', but I rouged my cheeks and lips when she was occupied with other things. Thus dressed, I descended the stairs at Hanover Street. Papa said I looked 'very well', which, as you know, dear sister, is high praise indeed. Heathcliff, who was also dressed for the occasion and did not look amiss despite his bearing, merely averted his eyes from me. I could not let that pass after our shared experience – he had ignored me for days. If he is to be my shadow, then I resolved to make him one, and asked him directly, in the haughtiest manner I could muster, 'Do you not approve of the ribbons and lace you took such delight in helping me choose?' He scowled and uttered something under his breath. I was about to continue when Papa interposed with his customary, 'Enough, Henrietta.' Chastised, I stepped back from Heathcliff, with no fond feelings towards him. However, my view of him was softened somewhat by the events of the evening, as you shall hear in due course. If only correspondence could be un-chronological, if that is a word, then I could inform you of events in the order of importance.

I will move on to our arrival at the ball. The Exchange, which so disgusted me, was entirely transformed. Do you recall our merry games at Speke, when we played at being faery folk? I remember well the walled garden: our land of sprites and pixies. Although I was grown, I still walked in our faery garden after you departed Speke, often in the morning, when the dew on the cobwebs reminded me of chandeliers. Entering the Exchange on the evening of the ball was akin to attending a gathering in our fanciful faery realm. I wish you could have been there, Charlotte, to see, so wonderfully, how our imaginary world was somehow rendered substantial.

The building's façade was adorned with colossal lamps and transparent paintings. Inside, the hard, masculine lines were diffused by the light of a thousand candles, formed into stars and festoons. Some very clever person had erected a roof over the quadrangle, creating another floor entirely. This upper room formed a grand saloon, brilliantly illuminated by lamps of every colour. I counted five polished metal chandeliers suspended from the ceiling, decorated with a multitude of stars, bathing the room with luminosity. There were four or five circular bars for the purpose of supplying refreshment. The concert and assembly halls were appropriated for dancing and had a most magical appearance when viewed from the saloon. Papa said it was the grandest spectacle ever seen in England, and that the lucidity of the building would pall even the palaces of France.

The same lucidity issued from the company – I have never seen such an elegant assembly, Charlotte! The ladies were in full dress and made at least three inches taller by their high-heeled shoes. I was quite the Lilliputian beside them, in my low-heels. I am certain Papa and Hana would have me remain a child forever, but women marry and have children younger than I am now.

However, despite Papa's best efforts, I did dance. He grew more distracted as the evening progressed, speaking at length with his associates, thus not choosing my dancing partners with his customary care. In consequence, several gentlemen asked to be introduced to me – two of whom were uncommonly handsome. One gentleman, who was not yet one-and-twenty, was a delightful dancer. He wore cannon curls, in the fashion of King

George, but they became him more than they do His Majesty in his portraits. Mr Thornton, for that was his name, was the son of a lord, therefore Papa approved and has since mentioned him again to me. I know what Papa is about, but Mr Thornton, though he was handsome and of good breeding, had little or no conversation. I attempted to engage him, questioning him on his preferred novels, the theatre, the places he would like to visit, and whether he enjoyed walking. His lack of interest in anything pleasing did not recommend him to me. He stated that as an eldest son and heir to a 'large fortune', he did not have time at his disposal for 'such frivolity'. I did not dance with him again, in defiance of his exquisite curls and twenty-thousand a year. What do I care about wealth? I doubt very much he is as moneyed or as well-connected as Papa.

This brings me to Heathcliff, and to an event that is still lengthening and unsettling my nights. Although Heathcliff's curls were not as exact as Mr Thornton's, they did not look amiss – indeed, I found them quite becoming, for they were his own. But despite his efforts to 'look the part', he was decidedly uncomfortable in both his surroundings and in the company he was expected to keep. He remained close to Papa, but he was occasionally dispatched to watch over me. I am afraid you will be vexed by my conduct, especially after he rescued me, putting himself at considerable risk. I cannot think of my behaviour without mortification. Here are the particulars – I entreated him, in jest, to dance a minuet, but he uttered an oath so terrible that the gentlemen in our vicinity ceased their conversations and gave Heathcliff a look that made it perfectly clear his position amongst them. They asked if the 'colt' was troubling me. I believe I blushed, not for the attentions of the gentlemen, but for my own conduct. For the first time, I felt pity for Heathcliff and regretted my cruelty terribly. I can be so careless; you have always said so. My jests had produced those oaths, and he had revealed himself to a company that could only look upon him with scorn. He did not cower however, he seemed to stand taller, and his eyes burned into the gentlemen, which they could not tolerate for long, and thus moved to another part of the assembly room. When I felt his eyes on me, I could not meet them, and he soon returned to Papa – leaving me alone on the edge of the minuet I had mockingly asked him to join.

I attempted to atone over dinner, by positioning myself next to him. The Mr Thorntons of the world could 'go to the deuce', as Heathcliff would say, although I blush to repeat that curse, even to you. Papa seemed to find the seating arrangement amusing and did not rebuke me. I can only surmise that Papa supposed I was plaguing him again, and Heathcliff's grim expression certainly imparted that impression. He did not wish to be near me – he made that evident to all. I was grateful for the distractions. The tables were arranged in such a manner that splendid and interesting objects presented themselves to every person: there was a device of Mercury bringing the joyful news of the king's recovery to Neptune; a transparency of the king's coat of arms; another transparency exhibiting an exact representation of the Exchange, illuminated in the same manner as on the night of the ball, with a full-length, robed image of the king in the interior. I pointed to these marvels and attempted to explain their significance to Heathcliff. His frown remained, but he did look at the ornaments with a degree of interest. He seemed unwilling to speak, more than usual, and I wondered if he felt humiliated, for our table was ringing with polite conversation.

The last hours of the ball were wretched for me. I endeavoured to make myself agreeable to him and he made it apparent that I was merely an annoyance to him. But I could not allow him to ruin an evening that had held so much expectation. I became nettlesome in my bad-temper – I named him blackguard and went in search of a more agreeable companion.

I danced three more dances, feigning equilibrium and good humour, and Papa, Heathcliff and I departed just as the sky began to lighten into morning. I felt weary in the coach – the sound of hooves on cobbles lulling me to sleep. I am still very much exhausted, and I occasionally squander a few hours reliving the star-filled faery realm of the ball. My reveries, however, are always broken by the memory of my conduct towards Heathcliff, and his subsequent mortification and anger.

Please do not chide me – I am resolved to be more pleasant to Heathcliff from now on.

Write soon, Charlotte.
Your loving sister,

Henrietta

Hanover Street, Liverpool – 16th June
Dearest Charlotte,

This is a very quick note to inform you of my plans regarding Heathcliff. After many hours of thought and concentration, I have settled on a design. To atone for my dreadful conduct, I will school him in elocution so that he may pass for a gentleman. Do you not think this idea capital? Clothes make the man, but an inappropriate accent can unravel all the tailor's good work.

I have not shared this design with him – I am certain he will not take exception at an enterprise that will be beneficial to him.

Yours, as ever,
Henrietta

Hanover Street, Liverpool – 22nd June
Dear Charlotte,

I must admit I was aggrieved by your last letter. To scold me not for cruelty, but for pitying and attempting to improve the life of a person 'beneath' me, was wholly unexpected and disappointing. You were always very kind to the servants in Speke, and Papa praises Heathcliff's service – why, dear sister, must I not also be compassionate towards him? He is a rough fellow, I admit, but I am certain his roughness proceeds from a life of toil and affliction. I am not making a 'pet' of him, as you so unfairly claimed in your letter.

There are several benevolent societies in Liverpool, many of which Papa is patron of. You must remember the Blue Coat School, which was established for the good of orphans and fatherless children. Papa visited the school two days ago and I was permitted to accompany him. I am sorry to have ever questioned Papa's character – please forget my request for information. I now see his worth clearly. He is a very generous benefactor; he funds lessons in reading, writing, and subjects as interesting as navigation and astronomy. Papa said that he often takes boys with an aptitude for sea-fare and makes sailors of them. The charity clothes, feeds, and lodges the poor children. Without Papa's aid, those children would become street urchins. Can you see, dear sister, that Heathcliff may have come from such an establishment? I want to be as kind and as useful as Papa to those in diminished circumstances. Heathcliff has risen, but his mode of speech will always reveal him for what he is: a member of the lower orders.

I do not wish to be cross with you – your letter made me feel wretched, and I feel the loss of your support keenly. Let us not argue, sister, for whom can I confide in if not you?

Your most affectionate sister,
Henrietta

Hanover Street, Liverpool – July 1st
My dearest Charlotte,

I was very much gratified by your letter, sister. I waited at home every morning for eight days, hurling myself down the stairs whenever Hana was summoned to the door, earning a reproachful 'shoo, girl!' for my efforts. Then this morning, finally, there was word from you. I was excessively concerned I had offended you, but your reply, although brief, did not contain the expected reprimand. For this, I thank you.

I have begun Heathcliff's education – not without some persuasion on my behalf. I spent days imagining and reimagining differing scenes. In one, Heathcliff reacted in his customary way: with oaths and curses and furious grinding of teeth. In another, I succumbed to wish fulfilment: I conceived Heathcliff thanking me and kissing my hand in gratitude, and although you will think me absurd, also in affection. Am I wrong, dear sister, to want a companion? Hana is becoming so tiresome – she lectures me endlessly and I long to be away from her. I do not understand the change in her, but whatever the reason for her transformation, she vexes me to the point of distraction. Heathcliff, regardless of his roughness and incivility, does not school me or attempt to alter the hue of my thoughts. He is a rare creature indeed.

After days of self-reflection and much deliberation, I settled upon a plan. I acquired a very useful publication written by a Mr William Enfield, called *The Speaker: Miscellaneous Pieces, Selected from the Best English Writers, and Disposed Under Proper Heads, with a View to Facilitate the Improvement of Youth in Reading and Speaking*. I am certain, Charlotte, it is the lengthiest title to be inflicted upon the world. I confess that I neglected many of the three hundred pages, but I did label three or four passages and copied the most useful exercises into a notebook. I was armed with this notebook and Mr Enfield's text, when I first summoned Heathcliff to my sitting room, four mornings ago.

I bade him sit, which he did, without complaint. The morning was a heavy grey – the meagre light within the room dispersed shadows into all the corners. Heathcliff chose one such corner to sit in, therefore I did not have full access to his shifts in mood. I decided to proceed regardless of the enforced distance between us.

I began with, 'I am so frightfully sorry about the events at the ball, Heathcliff. Those gentlemen were exceedingly ill-bred, even ungentlemanly. Your composure was a credit to you,' as I'd rehearsed. He made no reply to this compliment; he merely leaned back in his chair, moving further from the light. 'I have been thinking, Heathcliff, about how I could help you to avoid such mortifying scenes in future.' He sighed and made to stand. I motioned for him to remain seated. 'Miss Unsworth,' he began. 'Henrietta, please,' I interposed. 'Miss Unsworth,' he began again, 'I have errands to run for your father, I cannot sit here and be idle.' I saw my opportunity. 'I do not intend for you to be idle, Heathcliff.' I presented him with Mr Enfield's book. 'A book?' he asked, visibly perplexed. 'What do I want with a blasted book?' I sat nearer to him and tried to explain my plan. 'What you mean is: may I ask the purpose of this book?' He stared at me. 'You see, Heathcliff, I am going to teach you to speak like a gentleman, so that you will never be humiliated again.' I leaned back, smiling at him. He did not return the smile, not at first, but he stared most intensely at me for several moments. I felt bare beneath his gaze, but I met it regardless, despite the stir in my stomach. After a long silence, he smiled – not warmly exactly, but the smile revealed sufficient pleasure. 'Shall we begin now?' I asked him, suddenly feeling very shy. 'Aye,' he said, stopping and frowning slightly. 'Yes, Henrietta, let us begin.'

We have met every day since that morning – I am very pleased with his progress. He has begun to correct the nonsenses, the 'nowts' and 'ayes', that have littered his speech for so long and he has become almost companionable.

But this morning, Hana discovered our tête-à-tête, and proceeded to sit with us, whilst pretending to stitch a handkerchief. In her presence Heathcliff became taciturn once more and, in my vexation, I demanded that she leave the room. Hana informed me that it was her duty to remain. I was about to argue when Heathcliff suddenly arose and stood over her. I could not view Heathcliff's face, but I could see Hana's expression. She gripped the handkerchief and stared, unblinkingly, at Heathcliff. It was the strangest picture, Charlotte, neither person wished to look away. In the end, it was Hana who could bear it no longer. She had squeezed the handkerchief with such force, that the forgotten needle within its folds had lodged itself into the palm of her hand. She cried out and removed the needle; a blot of blood inked on the surface of her skin. I rose by instinct and went to attend her, whilst Heathcliff watched silently. When he spoke, both Hana and I started. 'Leave her, Henrietta,' he said. I was so cross with her, that I did as he asked, assuming that he would follow me into the hallway. When I turned, he informed me he would visit me later, and shut himself in the room with Hana.

I was anxious and very close to confiding the entire scheme to Papa, but Heathcliff found me in the library not long after and informed me that he had attempted to reason with Hana, to convince her of his good character. I cannot express my relief at this information, dear sister. I had imagined intrigue, betrayal, the stuff of novels, but Heathcliff is not the rough boy he once was. Through our elocution lessons, he is becoming civilized. I think you would like him now, Charlotte.

I have not seen Hana since this morning; I do not wish to see her. Heathcliff said he found her most unreasonable.

Tell me all your news, dearest sister.

Yours affectionately,
Henrietta

Hanover Street, Liverpool – 19th July
Dearest Charlotte,

I am exceedingly sorry for my tardiness. I received your first letter twelve days ago and your second on Tuesday – I have been so occupied that I am only now sitting down to write this reply. I am sorry you have been unwell. Is your cold improved now? Summer colds are more disobliging than their winter counterparts – I am certain of it. I hope John is taking pains to look after you. Inform me immediately if he is not attending to you – I shall send for a post-chaise and be with you before the week is over. Together, we will dare Papa's wrath!

Papa's enmity does not vex me, but I hope I have not earned your disapproval, Charlotte. I want to reassure you, once again, that your concern is unwarranted – Heathcliff is my pupil, and his progress has been swift. So, you see, dear sister, I am an accomplished teacher. Perhaps I will run away to become a governess! Imagine the scandal!

Papa noted the difference in Heathcliff over breakfast only the other day. He entered the morning room to deliver a letter to Papa, and his manner was so courteous and his accent so softened, that Papa said, 'I am not sure I like this new Heathcliff.' Papa uttered this in jest, and laughed heartily. I know Heathcliff does not like to be ridiculed, thus I expected him to lapse into surliness once more, but he smiled and bowed his head courteously, looking for me as he did so. Oh, Charlotte, I was so proud! My only regret is that his demeanour has improved so much that I can no longer laugh at him.

My derision has become a most profound and sincere sympathy. His struggles have become my struggles – I feel each slight, each unkind glance. Even Papa, who I know sees much in Heathcliff, jests most cruelly within his hearing. Hana cannot abide him. I have spent many an evening petitioning her to be kinder towards him. Strangers, I think, look upon him differently now, at least. The improvement in his speech has had the most remarkable effect on his person: he carries himself more upright; his scowl is smoothed almost into extinction; his manners are now those of a gentleman. I am encouraging him to read – to improve his mind and to furnish him with learned conversation. He seemed very reluctant, but I pressed upon him the importance of improving his mind: he now carries *Tom Jones* by Mr Fielding on his person. I found the novel coarse and did not finish it, but I thought Heathcliff would find much in common with the hero. In a similar vein, I have asked Papa to allow Heathcliff to accompany us to the theatre on Friday evening. We are to see a Shakespeare play – I forget which one. It would benefit Heathcliff greatly to witness it.

Do you recall when Papa took us to view *A Midsummer Night's Dream*? Do you think it became our favourite play simply because it was Mama's? I remember watching Mama more than the actors, for she was enraptured by it. She looked extremely well, didn't she? There was a gleam to her skin and a clarity to her eyes that I had never beheld before. We could not have known then that this lucidity was the illness' final cruelty. A fortnight, Charlotte. How could it only have taken a fortnight?

I am sorry for dwelling on the past, dear sister, but I have not attended the theatre since that evening eight years hence and the anticipation of it has made me pensive. I do hope Papa allows Heathcliff to attend, for I shall not grieve for times past if he is near.

I do hope you feel better presently, dear sister. Please remain warm indoors and alert me if you require my presence. I long to see you!

Yours affectionately,
Henrietta

Hanover Street, Liverpool – 29th July
Dearest Charlotte,

I am exceedingly glad of your recovery, and that you can roam again. Your garden sounds delightful; I hope I shall also walk amongst the hibiscus and honeysuckle one day.

I feel so strange, Charlotte: I cannot imagine remaining in Hanover Street, the world has shifted beneath me – I am adrift. It is difficult to explain. I am afraid of revealing too much. This feeling, for that is the only word I can think of to describe it, began on the evening we attended the theatre.

The theatre in Williamson-square is unchanged from when we attended *A Midsummer Night's Dream* with Mama and Papa all those years ago. I could not remember many details beforehand, but upon entering the theatre I remembered our last visit most vividly: the heavy doors that seemingly opened by magic; the chandelier blooming above the staircase; the chiming of a hundred conversations; Mama amongst it all, bright with consumption. If Heathcliff had not steadied me,

I believe I would have fainted. The sensation of his arm holding me firmly and his hand upon my waist anchored me to the present, and I was grateful to him. When he cast me off again, I was able to proceed with the appearance of equilibrium.

Papa hired a box for us – to the immediate right of the stage. The actors could be seen clearly, but we were high enough to remain separate from the play. I have heard of productions in which the actors acknowledge and address the audience – a prospect that filled me with dread. I did not wish to be seen by them, and Heathcliff, who had retreated into the folds of the curtain behind us, seemingly shared this dread.

Papa bade Heathcliff sit and explained to him that the actors were from London and at the end of the summer, they would return there. He pressed upon him the significance of his invitation, and that Heathcliff 'knew how to shew his gratitude'. I did not fully understand the exchange, but then the actors appeared on stage accompanied by thunder and lightning, and I forgot to enquire Papa's meaning. The play was *The Tempest* – the very storm seemed to be inside the theatre. The actors thrashed wildly on the stage as though besieged by vast waves. When the ship perished, and Miranda appeared, her dress bellowing and her hair aflame, I wanted to become her – to feel her pain at the loss of the ship's crew, to bear her distaste for her father's actions.

Can I trust you, Charlotte, to say nothing of what I am about to divulge? I call on our bond as sisters. If you can imagine ever breaking that bond, I must ask you not to read what follows and to destroy this letter immediately.

Heathcliff remained aloof, but when the monster Caliban appeared, he edged closer to the balcony, closer to me. I could sense him behind me. When Caliban cursed Prospero and Miranda, he exhaled, and I felt his breath – hot against the back of my neck. Papa missed a great deal of the play. His associates, including the mayor, continuously appeared to discuss business. Heathcliff and I were, therefore, alone a great deal but still in the company of the hundreds of people beneath us. The audience faded into nothingness, however, when Heathcliff needled a finger through an aperture in my chair, finding the space between my skirt and my bodice. He whispered the name 'Cathy'. I did not mind. I know you must wonder at this, Charlotte, particularly when you hear that I made no reply and was too surprised and confused to prevent him. Ferdinand and Miranda's love was being performed on the stage, and I did not wish to stop Heathcliff – not even when his lips pressed against my neck. But then the curtains opened behind me, and Heathcliff drew back; just as Papa returned to his seat, still discussing the rigging of a ship with an unknown associate who had followed him into our box.

I was discomposed, as you can imagine, and expected Heathcliff to act again, but instead he withdrew and when I turned to look at him, his eyes were fixed on the stage. Papa remained for the rest of the performance. I was so lost in thought that I barely remember the end of the play. I was grateful when Papa, just as we were about to leave, was approached by another associate who, with some urgency, entreated Papa to remain to discuss a shipment of some kind, therefore Heathcliff was to accompany me home in the carriage.

I have never felt so conscious, Charlotte. I barely breathed as we ascended the carriage, but Heathcliff seemed composed and cold as he sat opposite me. After a few moments of silence, I could bear it no longer. I asked him, 'Why did you kiss me, Heathcliff, only to be so unfeeling now?' He leaned forward so that our faces were inches apart. 'Would you like me to kiss you again?' I could not answer, and suddenly his hands were upon me, his mouth on mine. I pulled away briefly and asked him a question that I then regretted; I asked the identity of 'Cathy'. He moved away from me slightly, and said coldly, 'Do not utter her name.' I cannot go on, dear sister, only to say that he would not look upon me during what followed between us.

I am as culpable as Heathcliff; therefore I must entreat you once again, Charlotte — please do not speak of what I have revealed to you. Papa would destroy Heathcliff, and I am as much to blame as he is. I know he is beneath me, and that his conduct on the evening of the play was questionable, but there is also nobility within him, that he conceals from the world. I am no longer a child, Charlotte. I can check Heathcliff's behaviour if I need to. I am in love with him — I am certain of it.

Yours affectionately,
Henrietta

Hanover Street, Liverpool — 24th August
Dearest Charlotte,

I am undone…

Hana

Liverpool
August 1782

Heathcliff. Heath cliff. He.

He a curse on my lip, in my mouth, in my throat. He give me the bellyache I wish on him. He red eboe, white nigger become massa, crawling like centipede, cockroach in my gut. He anansi, orb weaver, his web strong, and she tied up. Nobody know, nobody know she tied, she trapped, not Massa Unsworth, his daughter gone, his daughter lost, and he not know. Hana know, Hana see. Hana see him before in other form, other place. He devil, he contagion, and he no boy.

He no boy, I say to Miss Henrietta, he devil set to ruin you. You hear me?

She laugh, I tell too many story, sing too many song about ruin and strife, I think bad thought she say.

Listen, child, I say, he no good, he insect that infect and rot them he feed on.

Her laughter run dry and she look at me with eye that is not hers. Do not make her choose, she say, he save her while I indisposed, she say, and would not attend her. There good in him, she say.

Indisposed, she say. Ind is posed. Posed.

I pose to you, miss, that he got design, that he no hero.

She lift her head and sigh to heaven. She tell me to go about my work, to let her be. How can I let her be? She like my child, and my love deep, as deep as well water.

In voice that not hers, she scream for me to get out, to leave her. She call me slave and I cry, cry in patois, that the Heathcliff-devil has her, my Henrietta, my sweet, sweet child.

He change her. He change everything.

I serve Massa Unsworth for twenty five year. He bring me from Jamaica as child and make me lady-maid to Missus Unsworth, his bride. She kind but of simple understanding, she not see Massa Unsworth's heat for me, his need for my warm, slave cunt. My child cunt. He bring me across ocean for it.

The sea voyage nearly kill me. Massa Unsworth bring me to cabin, save me from disease in bowel of ship. He find me with my mama, her eye and finger a feast for rat. He pull me away and I scream, for I know his plan, and with no mama, he be my papa and my mate. I stay in cabin, sleep naked on rug at his feet. When I cry all night, he tell me he make me better. His hand cold and then wet-warm and when I hurt no more, I sleep.

Massa Unsworth speak of pleasure and pain, that both same thing.

I see no truth in that. I see no pleasure in pain taking or pain making, but men, they different. I try teach this to Miss Henrietta, but she lonely, she simple heart, and she not know her papa. She trust him as she trust He-devil.

Missus Unsworth die of fever, and I now both mother to Miss Charlotte and Miss Henrietta and whore to their papa. Nearly every child of my own be beat out of me, so they only children I got.

Miss Charlotte got eye open and she see her papa's weakness.

She ask me how many year he visit me.

I look at my feet. I make no answer. Miss Charlotte hold my shoulder and she shake me until my teeth rattle.

She say I must answer, she has right to know.

I shake my head and tell her I sorry for her mama's passing.

She angry and tell me to leave Speke.

I tell her I nowhere to go.

She say I can go to hell, die on street, return to Jamaica.

I wretched, I love Miss Charlotte and cannot tell her truth.

I go see Massa, and ask for freedom, to go home, to return to singing cricket and chirping tree frog. He angry, he tell Miss Charlotte she silly girl, she need occupation, she need distraction. They do not speak for week and by end of month,

Miss Charlotte to marry gentleman. Miss Henrietta say she bereft, she cry and wring hand, she question and go mad, but she not receive answer, she not receive comfort. I stay close and soothe her like she baby and run when Miss Charlotte be near.

Massa Unsworth not pay me visit until Miss Charlotte gone.

After many year of service, of his needle in my cunt, of children dead before alive, I not beg for freedom again.

Miss Henrietta, sweeter than Miss Charlotte. She be mine and I her happy companion in bitterness. She hate Speke, she hate her papa for he keep her there, she hate sister for leaving. I try convince her to settle, but she want life, she want Liverpool. I want slumber, I want to see Massa once in while, not every day. I want bitterness to take suck, and to grow strong in quiet place.

Hana want Miss Henrietta to herself, but Hana no say, no claim on nobody.

Liverpool be misery to me. The dock, the dirty street, the tall ship with rat and disease and death. In twenty five year there new dock, more tall ship, more death, and at Hanover Street, Massa Unsworth give me room next to him, not next to Miss Henrietta and I know how thing work. At night, I his, but in daytime, I hers, and there more hour in day than night, so my bitterness sleep.

Miss Henrietta happy and I happy for her, but then He-devil take her away, and I angry, I fury.

We walk and walk in daytime, some street familiar and some change so much I not recognise any building. She like the dock, the dark street that reek of piss, the poorhouse. I think she want to forget Speke, that why she drawn to ill-natured place. Bad men watch her and look at her woman breasts, and I afraid and tell Massa Unsworth that Miss Henrietta woman now.

I sorry for telling Massa. Next day, the He-devil attend us, he creep and trail like weed. He watch Henrietta and look away when she look at him, and he realise I see everything, and he hate me. He hate me because I black nigger, I no half-breed bitch. I nigger bitch cause that what Massa call me. What he say I am, I am.

Miss Henrietta care not for He-devil, and I not worry until I take to bed, and cannot watch over her.

Miss Henrietta blame me for what happen, she think I have English cold, that I weak little girl not woman.

I not see her for six day, as baby bleed out me. My mama teach me obeah before she die on ship, and I mix herb, fennel and cotton root and clary sage. I not find motheroot or juniper here, but potion still strong. Massa Unsworth wait for herb to work before he beat me. Two day of pain and purge, I yield baby clot. I wrap it and burn it on fire, then I lie with towel between thigh and sleep, too weak for worry. On fourth day, Massa enter with club and ask if I need it.

Baby gone, I say, but I sick, I still bleed.

He fetch doctor, he say, I done well, he say.

He tell me to wash myself, and water get carried to room with soap. I think he love me and I smile, but the club, I nearly die of Massa's club...

I hope he leave me recover, rest, grow strong, but he weak and on me before blood dry inside me.

I disgust him, he tell me.

When I see Miss Henrietta, she flush with danger, she speak of bad man and Heathcliff, and head separate from body in earth. I not see how head still alive and she laugh, but I see with clear eye the change in her and the new way she speak of He-devil.

I call him centipede, spider, but she not see. She not try to see.

I beg Massa Unsworth to attend grand ball with Miss Henrietta, to watch over her, but he say I have idea above myself, that I nigger slave, that he treat me too well. He send for Heathcliff devil and he watch as Massa beat me with stick from fire. I want to spit at He-devil, tear his flesh, beat him with stick, but he wear white clothes and stand tall. The He-devil see my fury and ask to beat me too, but Massa say no, I his slave.

I agony and full of poison, but when I see Miss Henrietta, I walk up and right, smile and do not cry. She bid me upstairs and I help her dress. I try to make her child again, with no heel or rouge, so He-devil and no other man take notice of her. But she still beautiful, she still near full bloom. I tell her be careful, not to trust He-devil, but she distract with own beauty, and she not listen to warning.

I not rest until carriage arrive with Miss Henrietta inside.

I pace house, sore still after Massa's stick, but I not get caught idle. I scrub floor, polish glass, prepare fireplace for morning, tidy Miss Henrietta's chamber and when all done, and clock chime three time, I sit near window and watch for her. Night be thick and quiet, with mist under window, and a chill in air.

I like night in Jamaica more than loneliness and coldness of English night.

In Jamaica me never alone. There always roar of sea, of cricket song in forest, warm candle and lantern hanging bright from veranda, my mama's song. Jamaica safe place, until white man come back and bring nigger ship from Africa and start clear land and build grand house and steal Jamaica children. I still not know why Massa Unsworth choose us, why my cunt so fine, finer than Missus

Unsworth's. My papa and brother he whipped and work on plantation and mama lie back with leg force open by Massa Unsworth while our home burn down. After, I and mama taken to harbour and then for many week, an endless night of sea, sea, sea.

The memory of Jamaica be comfort and I sleep in chair and wake at sound of carriage outside. The sky burn and I must be up in hour. I watch Miss Henrietta's sleeping face as she get carried into house, and I steal up for bed. I do not wish visit from Massa. I put chair under door handle. I know he angry, but after he beat me, he sometime kind. I take risk and pretend not hear when footstep stop outside door. I pretend not hear when he try handle and swear at me.

I lie still as moth and wait for light.

Miss Henrietta sleep all morning away, and Massa Unsworth and He-devil leave house in hurry. I stay out of sight until they gone, and then I go to Miss Henrietta. She not want disturbing, but I curious about ball.

Come, Miss Henrietta, I say, it will soon be night and you not sleep unless you dress now. She sit at desk and flick me away with hand. I be no insect, Miss Henrietta, I say.

Go away, she say, and order me to leave room.

I go, I say, but Hana worry about you. Hana wait all night for you, for sound of carriage.

Miss Henrietta turn from desk and cry.

Oh, Hana, she say, she sorry for sending me away, she wretched and it not my fault.

I ask about grand ball, and she cry more. I sit on edge of bed, and she tell me she behave badly to He-devil. She say he not talk to her no more, and she angry with herself. I make noise of sympathy, but in my heart, I rejoice and thank lord and obeah god for saving my sweet girl.

But my rejoice is short as English winter day.

She got trouble, she think hard, she write list and write letter to Miss Charlotte, and I a fool. My girl got plan, she for turning He-devil into pet, but he no pet, he savage and he tame in look only. I speak her this, and she sigh and try send me away.

I tell her she not send me away, I know her since baby, I help her mama birth her.

She say she grown now, she not need me.

You hurt me, hurt me, here, I say, and press where heart be.

She sigh and send me away, and this time, I go.

But I not go far. I worry and fret and watch. When door open at night and Massa Unsworth climb on me, I worry and fret, and once he gone, I watch. Nigger good at watching, at hiding, at avoiding whip or hand, but I not good as some. I high idea of myself and I happily get whip for Miss Henrietta, but I need more than Hana-feeling to prove he He-devil.

I watch for week, two week. I watch Miss Henrietta teach him language, language he use to curse me with. He call me thick-lip, I tell him his lip nearly thick as mine. He see me watching, and he whisper whore as I pass, he grab at my swollen breast, he say maybe he knock on my door one night, see where he come from. I not understand, but I know danger, I know he beast of prey, but I know how to trap beast in forest.

I sit with Miss Henrietta and He-devil when she teach him. I take sewing so I not look at them. I feel his devil fury and Miss Henrietta's anger.

She stand and tell me leave.

I say, it my duty to stay, miss.

She about to speak again, but He-devil rise and she step aside for him. I not look away from his black eye. His eye be marble like fireplace in dining room, like blackness of sea at night, but I know darkness, and I not look away from it. I curse him in silence, in my head, I picture blister on body, I picture needle in heart, and he know, he know what I hope, and he smile, his tongue a lash that curl over lip, teeth, over my curse. I not feel needle at first, I focus on curse and forget what I hold until needle is half inch into my palm and handkerchief turn red. I look away from He-devil, and Miss Henrietta, still with kind heart, come help me. But He-devil be massa now and he send Miss Henrietta from room.

When door close, he strike my face.

He grip me, tell me not to make sound.

I remember Massa Unsworth call me his, his slave, he never share me, and I think of trap.

I ask He-devil what he want with Miss Henrietta, she little girl, why he want girl when he can get woman. In my head I see Massa Unsworth walk into bedroom and see He-devil on me. He beat He-devil and send him out of house, and Miss Henrietta never see him again.

His grip get loose and he look at me different. I think my trap working, that he soon gone, but then he say he not care for Miss Henrietta or me, he care only for place call Heights. He return home, he say, rich and make terrible revenge. He-devil look away from me, and I confused.

It most he ever speak to me, and I not know what say.

While I think, he speak again.

Do not think to trap him with promise for fuck, he say, I fool if think he want me when he grab my breast, a breast he may have suckle when baby. He hate me and what is between my leg.

You never suckle woman breast, I say, you suckle devil's tit.

He sigh and say he got plan, that if Hana stay in his way, he tell Massa Unsworth Hana offer him her sweet slave cunt. I know what Massa Unsworth do, He-devil say, I know he kill me. I his slave, he say, and Massa Unsworth not like to share.

I hate He-devil, I curse him, I spit in his face. He wipe it and warn me to stay away from Miss Henrietta, to let him have own way.

Hana not stay away, Hana love Miss Henrietta, I say.

Do you know what happen to slave whore when they unfaithful to massa? he ask.

I stay still and look him straight.

He hear many story in English colony, he say, when women be bury to neck and the massa command other slave to throw stone after stone at woman's head. He smile and ask if I know what happen next.

I know how it end, I say.

He nod and tell me anyway. There be nothing left of head, he say, just bone and brain, and then he quickly grab my head and he squeeze until I cry out.

Do I see? he ask, still with tight hold. It like breaking egg shell, he say.

I writhe and squirm like fish on hook, then he let go and I run for door.

The hallway be quiet. I think of He-devil and what he say, and I think it all a dream. I think he got no power, but then I think of Massa Unsworth throwing stone at my head, and I sit on stair and cry in handkerchief, handkerchief still red from needle. I wish it his blood. I wish he dead. He say he suckle my breast, I say he no woman's baby. I curse him with obeah and pray to white god for strength to defeat this devil. This devil in boy form.

Miss Henrietta ask what pass between He-devil and I as I fix her hair and make dress ready for show.

She tell me it not show, it play.

I not understand, and she irritable.

It story, she say, for act out on stage, a play, by William Shakespeare.

I not know Massa William, I say, and she sigh. I tell you story, I say.

No, she say, she not want my story, I no Shakespeare, she say.

I fix her hair in silence, and she ask me what He-devil say, and she tell me not call him He-devil, his name Heathcliff.

I not speak truth, for she not believe truth, she not want to hear realness, that he brute, he beast, that He-devil go to Massa

Unsworth with lie if I speak my fear. Hana not sure, Hana think before answer. Hana decide to say nothing.

Miss Henrietta say, tell me answer.

I shake my head no.

She look at me, and she look nervous for first time.

She insist I tell her, she say, she got right to know.

I shall not, miss, I say. I shall not tell.

She look back in mirror and she say, cold, that He-devil come to Massa William's play, and she ask him for truth of matter. She look at me through mirror, and I try keep face still.

I cannot work through her, I must wait for He-devil to act, and then I go to Massa. If Massa beat me, he beat me, but least I warn him, at least he approach and ask her. She not lie to her papa, Hana sure, she sweet girl still.

But He-devil move fast like cockroach, and Hana move too slow.

In morning, I ask Miss Henrietta if she like play.

She not look up from letter she writing.

I look and see Miss Charlotte's name. How is Miss Charlotte? I ask.

She say nothing. She write so fast her shoulder shake.

I try hold Miss Henrietta steady but she flinch when I put hand on her.

Get away, she scream, her eye big and dull like pebble. When she see my horror, she remember Hana, and she say sorry, she need just finish letter and then she send for me.

I nod and leave room, my heart heavy and my head full.

I seek He-devil, but he with Massa Unsworth in study. I listen at door and hear him in new language, speak like gentleman, about plantation, about many dead slave, not enough cotton arrive, foreman weak, more nigger needed. I know he talk of Jamaica plantation, and in my head I see father and brother dead in ditch and wonder how they dead, if they feel pain or if they dead before pain.

There be third person in room, I not know him, but his voice low and deep like valley. I afraid but want to see man, so I fetch water and brush, and scrub staircase outside Massa's study. When I finish, I start again, and when door open I not stop, but I eye man with voice like valley. He tall and white and look like important man.

He see me, and he say to Massa Unsworth, you keep a nigger here.

Massa tell him like I not hear, that I Maroon, that I and other Maroon think we born free, that I good use and soon all grand house in England have nigger slave. He not able to beat or fuck English maid, he say, but he do what he want with own property.

Tall man laugh, and put hand on Massa's back.

I look at step and the black smear of my face, and then I scrub, scrub it away.

She spend many day in room; she wait for He-devil, I sure of it. She not want to walk in town now, she say she tired and need rest. When Massa Unsworth not in Hanover Street, she take supper in own room. When I clean plate, she always in bed, in sleep. But I also try to pretend sleep, so I know when Miss Henrietta do same. She look like she not sleep for week and I know reason, and I plan and plan trap.

When Massa Unsworth go away for week, Heathcliff ask to stay in Hanover Street, I know it my chance to watch. I watch Miss Henrietta and He-devil from the dark and I not open mouth. I wait in shadow like spider.

On first night, I say I go to bed early, and clear plate. She smile and then hide it with frown.

Am I unwell, she ask.

No, Miss Henrietta, I say, Hana tired that all.

Very well, she say, rest, and she see Hana in the morning.

I nod and leave room with tray.

I take tray to kitchen and give to cook. She never speak and never look at Hana, but this time she ask if Miss Henrietta well.

I want tell truth, that she lost. But cook still not look Hana in face, and I say, yes, missus, she well, and I leave warm kitchen and begin night of long watch.

I move slow like anansi to room next to Miss Henrietta. There be bed with no blanket, no pillow, and there no curtain so cold moon fill room. This room mine if Massa not want me close. I sleep near Henrietta in Speke, and we like mother and child, now we not close, we not talk, and she has secret. I not sit on bed, I wait near door, and listen. When clock chime nine time, I hear movement on stair and I press ear on door. A floorboard creak and Miss Henrietta's door open and close like pitcher plant. I move to wall, and listen, but wall so thick or they so quiet. I hear nothing and want make bang on wall like madwoman, to run into room and kill He-devil with own hand, but I sit on floor and make only sadness, for I nigger, I nothing, and in truth I got no plan.

I sleep bad and cry. Hana weak, and Miss Henrietta gone too far for saving.

I attend her in morning like adopi, like ghost. I say nothing for many minute, and then see she look pale and I worry.

Are you well? I ask.

She look at me with watery eye and she shake head.

This first time she admit something wrong, so I sit on edge of bed and reach for her. It surprise when after moment, she bury head in me and she allow me to hold her.

Miss Henrietta, I say, as she sob, tell Hana how she help.

She sit up and rub eye.

Tell how Hana help, I say again.

Hana not able to help, she say, I not approve her choice and I tell her papa, she not trust me, she say.

This deep hurt, I say, I love Miss Henrietta, I say, it He-devil

I hate, but know Massa Unsworth also blind to truth. I hold Miss Henrietta's face and tell her I keep her secret if she tell me.

Miss Henrietta shake with sob and tell me to not name him He-devil, and she not able to say secret, it too terrible.

Can Hana say secret to you? I ask.

She look surprise, but she nod head.

You think you in love with Heathcliff, I say, and now his child be inside you.

How, she ask, how can Hana know?

I watch, I say, I listen. I try warn of danger many time. I know that danger, I say.

And now it too late, she says.

Heathcliff, I say, he know about baby?

Miss Henrietta nod and she sob again.

What he say? I ask.

Once she able, she say he quiet and curse baby. He want nothing with baby brat or her. She alone, she say.

I tell her she not alone, that I talk with Heathcliff, that there still six day until Massa Unsworth home.

I leave her in bad state and search for He-devil. I think of sending word to Massa Unsworth, but she trust me, and he not marry her to gentleman if he know truth, he send her back to Speke and lock her away from world. He kill He-devil but he also kill Miss Henrietta, in different way.

He-devil be nowhere, not in Massa's study, not in parlour, not in sitting room, not in kitchen, I even try He-devil's chamber, he disappear, he nowhere. I return to own room, I need place to think.

When I open door, I shock and feel sick, for He-devil sit on bed.

You have no right, I say, this my room, only Massa Unsworth allowed here. I not got much right, but I some, and no He-devil allowed in Hana's room.

Hana has no right, he say, Hana nigger slave and he beat idea of right and wrong out of me, if I think superior.

I lower head and curse him in mind. He dark on outside, white on inside.

He sigh and say, he not come to harass me, he come to discover if Hana love Miss Henrietta.

I raise head and look him in eye.

He-devil look away this time, in shame. He not all powerful.

She with child, he say, a bastard, if child live it grow up in hell.

What He-devil ask? I say.

He ask that I rid Miss Henrietta of burden, that I be dutiful servant, that I show love for her. He know Hana want him dead, he say, but does Hana want Miss Henrietta's ruin too?

Before I answer, he say he go to Africa and then Jamaica, he not know how long for. His black eye find mine. He not leave bastard brat here, he say, like Hana left him.

Like Hana left you? I say.

He-devil look at Hana with hatred, and I now know why.

Hana not your mama, I say, no child ever live, fifteen baby dead, I say. My hand rest on empty belly.

He-devil shake head and then nod, his breath heavy.

If Hana not help Miss Henrietta, he say like last moment never happen, he take miss by hair and throw her down stair. That his way for solve problem of bastard.

Then He-devil look tired. He rub his brow and he look young, a boy.

He a bastard, he say, he beaten and made low, and he not want another bastard in world.

I study He-devil for many moment. He fix his eye on corner of room, he far away. He seek his mama, but he hate her. She make pact with devil, for he not boy, not nigger, not white, some other thing. He abomination. Some would pity him for his poor orphan past, and maybe think he try to do good by ridding world of bastard child, but Hana known many man like him and my heart hard as Massa's club.

I not care for you, devil, I say, your mama cast you aside like waste. Massa Unsworth see you dead if he find daughter with baby, you no longer his favourite and there no voyage to Jamaica, you sink to bottom of sea, and you bastard so nobody care. Hana want that fate for you.

He look me in eye but he not move from bed.

I hate you, I say again, but you lucky, for I love Henrietta more than I hate you, and I not see her ruin and without husband, that why I do what you ask, I say.

He close his eye and breathe deep. He happy and I wretched.

I not help for your sake, I say, I hope ship that carry you sink in dark ocean. It fate you deserve and I curse and pray you drown.

He-devil laugh. He rid self of boy disguise.

Unsworth back soon, he say, how long it take?

She sick for week, I say, but it her first, so blood stop in three or four day.

Does Hana need more herb? he ask.

I tell him no, that he not needed, that he stay away. Miss Henrietta need god now, not devil.

I think he plan to quarrel, but he change mind, and he leave room. I hear his step on stair and know Miss Henrietta safe.

Once he gone, I take herb box from under bed. Cotton, clary sage, fennel. No motheroot, which make passage smooth. It not easy for Miss Henrietta and it pain me. It hurt in breast and in belly my sorrow for what she suffer.

What he say? she ask when I enter room. And what that in my hand?

I place box on table and sit on bed. Miss Henrietta look like child, with hair free over shoulder. Her eye wide and her lip quiver like kora string.

I tell her Heathcliff not want baby, and he not marry her. He go to colony, I say, he be gone long time.

She cry and pull own hair out.

Miss, I say, and I hold her down so she not harm self. Hana help you, Hana take baby away, your papa never know, I say.

How? she ask. Her life over.

No, miss, I say, it between us, this secret, you will marry, you have other child. You make good match.

She look at me with child eyes. It hurt? she ask.

I not lie to her. Yes, I say, but birthing full child hurt more.

She look at me strange, and I fear I talk too much, but she not ask yet. She wait.

The box, she say, what in the box?

I take out herb bottle and tell her name of each. I tell her I mix herb with water and she drink it, she drink every hour until her belly ache and she bleed out baby.

It not real baby, I say, it not long inside belly. Miss Henrietta hurt for some time and get weak, but Hana look after her, I say.

When she cry again, I tell her there no choice, and she brave girl, she get better and she forget Heathcliff. He bring pain to her, he no good.

She a fool, she say, she see that now and she sorry for it.

I tell her I go make potion and I leave room with wide smile. I show teeth and I say all is well, but I afraid for miss.

Potion take time to work, and Miss Henrietta sweat so much I worry baby come out that way.

On second day, her belly swell, and I see herb working. Miss afraid and she speak of death. I tell her she plenty of life for enjoy, she not die, and she calm for moment.

How does Hana know, she ask, how does Hana know she not die?

Am I dead, miss? I ask.

But who and when, she ask, she never see me with child.

I know she think and wonder about father of child, but I not tell her truth.

It before you born, miss, before England.

She narrow eye and almost speak when belly cramp take her and she gone elsewhere for time. When cramp gone she back with me, but there no more talk of my children, for her child bleed out of her, a dark, black blood that bloom on bedsheet like begonia.

Hana, she say, Hana, and then she faint away.

When I wake her with smelling salt, I put thick cloth of cotton between leg and clean bed. Old bedsheet I put in fire.

That worst of it, I say, your belly soft and you bleed a little every day and take rest. When bleed stop, you get up and take air.

She look at me and hold my hand. She squeeze it in thanks.

Hana love you, I say, you like daughter.

And Heathcliff, she say, where is he?

I see him far away, I say, in garden or in your papa's study, he not come up here. Hana sorry, I say, but he gone soon and you rid of him now.

She nod and look brave, but her heart be broken and her youth gone.

On third day of bleed, letter arrive for Miss Henrietta.

It from Charlotte, and I sick with worry. I think all well, but with letter from Miss Charlotte, I see we not alone, Hanover Street not world, and time and world outside still there.

I rush up stair to miss. I not think of Miss Charlotte and the letter Miss Henrietta write her, I slowwitted slave, distracted by He-devil. I forget Miss Henrietta always write and I think she must write truth to sister and I afraid.

I enter room without knock and fly at bed.

Hana, she say, she sit up, what the matter?

The letter you write, miss, I worry bad if you let Miss Charlotte know what trouble you.

She reach for drawer in bedside table, but she still sore, and she ask me open it. She tell me take out letter. It for Miss Charlotte.

She say she tell everything in last letter she write. She plan to send it, she say, but something stop her.

In head I thank English god Miss Charlotte not know, but I keep thought for me. I glad, I say to Miss Henrietta, nobody else know about baby.

I hand her new letter from Miss Charlotte and fetch clean cloth. I fold cloth and fold it until it tight, while miss read letter. When I ready to change dirty cloth, I look at miss and see she weep. She not make sound, but she clutch letter and sob, and paper crumple like handkerchief in hand.

Miss, I say, be Miss Charlotte sick?

She shake her head and try control breathing.

It worse, she say between breath, she with child. I not breathe, Hana, she say, I not breathe.

She hold at throat and she gasp for air. I hold and rock her and tell her breathe deep and slow, deep and slow.

I want to tell her she have child one day with good gentleman, that she forget He-devil and baby. But then fury rise in me.

She not Miss Henrietta now, not girl that talk and dance and laugh with gleam in eye. She broken, while cockroach devil begin new life, he come back gentleman and he marry into good family, and he hide low nature behind gentleman's clothes and gentleman's speech, and he break more girl, break them like wine glass on floor after he drink their health.

Hana not let him. Hana not let him.

I hold Miss Henrietta close and rock her, and with every pitch, I repeat oath to obeah god, to English god, my mama and her mama's adopi, to kill He-devil before he get on ship, before he change form and name.

He-devil. He. Heath cliff. Heathcliff.

I kill him before he become Massa.

Dr John Avery

on board the *Othello*
January – April 1783

January 1st

I did not seek to document, in detail, the *Othello*'s voyage during the three months of inaction and idleness that followed our departure from Liverpool; however, I am now compelled to write, and to write the truth, as I perceive it.

We landed in Sierra Leone this morning, on New Year's Day of all days, after a dreadful journey over the lip of West Africa. The brave vessel was battered on both sides as high as the topmast. The crew, all thirty of us, clung to ropes and to each other like swimmers near-drowning. The captain steered the ship through the storm as best he could, but as the prow lifted, like the tail of a great whale, some men could no longer hold on. They slid down the deck and were swallowed by the sea.

Captain Gunning had boasted, not two days before, that he had navigated many tempests, that storms habitually gather on this coastline like armies, but up until the waves had gradually decreased in size and the ship had slowly straightened, I admit that I had very little faith in him. In the end, the storm blew itself out as quickly as it had commenced. The sky, which was a cauldron of black cloud and rain, was suddenly a placid blue with a smudge of pale cloud, and the vessel, to my amazement, was intact.

I collapsed on deck almost instantly, my hands raw and my clothes crusted with salt water and vomit. I am not a natural seaman. I have been plagued with seasickness these last three months, much to the captain's contempt, but I had never known such exhilaration to be alive, to have survived when I thought all would be lost. My relief seemed to offend the captain, or perhaps it was the miracle of my survival that galled him, for after counting the crew he discovered the loss of four good seamen, one only a boy, decreasing our company to twenty-six souls, with still the Atlantic to cross. But after the storm had cleared and we gathered ourselves, we could see the coast of Sierra Leone. The sight of the verdant forests, of a green unseen in England, seemed to cheer the crew, many of whom had never ventured beyond the Irish Sea before this voyage. I marvelled at this strange country that had delivered me from near-death. I have suffered three months at sea and the sight of land was as welcome to me as a homecoming.

But the tempest had taken its toll; feeling suddenly vertiginous, I turned from the view and looked up at the clear sky. I closed my eyes, yet the sun still bled through my lids, and I wondered if we had collectively imagined the storm, a shared consciousness after long months at sea. But the dead are still dead; they are not returned.

When I opened my eyes, black flecks floated across my retinas and then multiplied until my vision was nearly entirely obscured. I shut my eyes again and turned away from the sun. When I opened them, the darkness was still all consuming. I breathed deeply, and thinking I was on the verge of fainting, groped for a handrail and slumped against it, my legs weak and my blood pounding in my ears. Eventually, after an effort, I willed the inky blotches away until my vision slowly returned. I squinted at the brightness of the African morning and did not notice the captain until he was standing directly over me.

I knew from his countenance that he meant to goad me. I have grown accustomed to his caprices these last few months, and for a time I chose not to hear him. Now, I must hear every insult, every cruelty, and record them in this journal. I must bear witness.

'Are you well, Doctor? It would be a disaster for the crew if *you* were to perish,' he said, his tone derisive. I informed him I was perfectly well and then we slipped into silence, for I knew his enmity. I was just about to express a wish of returning to my cabin when Gunning sighed deeply and, placing his hands on my shoulders, steered me towards the prow.

'I hate this place,' he said, once he'd positioned me to his satisfaction, his eyes fixed on the nearing shoreline. 'But I hate the people more. If you could *call* them people, of course.' I stared beyond the prow to the blue-green sea, the colour of a blackbird's egg, and the white beach, lined with thick trees. I wondered if this could be a paradise, but I knew better than to appear whimsical before the captain. Instead, I turned to him, and said, 'I have not met any Africans, and so I must reserve my judgement.' I regretted my seriousness almost instantly, since it would not be beneficial to make an open enemy of him, and tried to make light of the conversation, complaining of the 'damned heat', and how it might affect my opinion of the continent. He grinned at this and said that I will find 'the inhabitants as distasteful as the climate.'

We stood side by side for I know not how long, until the place I had named paradise was corrupted and tainted by the scene that awaited us at port. I have not sailed into many harbours in my thirty-five years on this earth, but I cannot imagine a worse seaport than that which awaited us in Sierra Leone. There were three or four other vessels moored, one ship as large as the *Othello*; the captain cursed and pronounced that the best slaves would be already purchased, and we must wait for more unfortunates to be brought from inland – a 'fresh stock', to use his words. There were lines of black figures on the quayside, all naked with their hands tied, all manacled around the neck and attached to each other by a long rod. Most stood erect, and the ones that did not were threatened with the lash. My face must have revealed my horror, for the captain laughed, 'not what you were expecting, Doctor?' I turned to answer him, but the words would not come. I had been struck dumb.

I watched as one line moved like a convoy of ants onto a ship named *The Maria*, an old Bristol frigate turned slaver, I discovered later. Even from a distance, it was clear that some, in fear or in refusal of what was to come, fought against their chains and attempted to run. These rebels were beaten and kicked by other Negroes, distinguishable from the slaves by their clothing, and then inadvertently dragged by the other slaves situated at the front of the line. They had no choice but to stand. As much as I could tell, those who ceased walking were in danger of being strangled by the neck clasp. I supposed this was a chain gang, but there were a hundred Negroes attached to each other, more perhaps – a figure that went beyond my worst suppositions when I prepared for this undertaking. I had only seen one set of chains before, displayed on the wall of my lodgings prior to my departure from Liverpool. There were twelve neck manacles in all, a number I remember thinking monstrous, but now, having seen a chain gang with ten times that number, my notion of what constitutes barbarism has altered.

I cannot pretend to know what drives the slaver to forsake his sense of pity, to forsake his own humanity, but I must make it my business to apprehend the darkness at the heart of this trade and contribute to its obliteration.

January 2nd

Before I attempt to document our first days of commerce in this hellish harbour, the character of the crew must be established, and an explanation of how I came amongst them should also be provided if my journal is to prove useful.

I travelled to Liverpool by post-chaise on September 1st. Reaching a strange town at night often leaves a lasting impression, and after a long journey from Norwich, I arrived in Liverpool with a sense of foreboding that I was unable to dispel. I am a rational man; I know my feeling that evening was the result of over-tiredness, as well as disappointment in my accommodation, but this sense of threat is still with me despite my removal from that odious lodging-place.

My accommodation was provided by the captain, James Gunning, and I remember thinking his taste was not refined, for it was a miserable establishment; now that I know more of him, I realise that his choice of lodgings reflected his character more deeply than I could ever have surmised on that first evening.

Madoc House, as it was called, had the advantage of location, for it was situated very close to the quayside of the Old Dock, but the landlady's attentions were stifling, and I do not have the talent of humouring persons I have no interest in. The house did have a comfortable hearth, but the other rooms were neglected, and the proximity of the Old Dock, although favourable during the day, proved a nuisance at night. The sailors, with no occupation whilst the ships remained in dock, turned to drink and revelry, and who could blame them? Nearly all sailors slept on the deck of their respective ships, and I am sure the rum kept them warm when they would otherwise have frozen.

I remained in Madoc House for a fortnight, whilst Captain Gunning waited for a favourable wind. I met with him numerous times during those weeks, and my impression of him did not improve upon further acquaintance. I hoped to find him sympathetic and sensitive to the plight of the Negroes, but this was his fourth voyage, and his concern for the slaves only extended to keeping them alive long enough to reach Kingston; I hid my approbation, as I knew I should, but I made notes of our conversations when I was alone.

During our first meeting, when I had planned to ascertain his values and opinions, he instead scrutinised *my* views most keenly. This reversal wrong-footed me and increased my sense of unease. My record as a doctor, prior to this commission, is a source of vexation that I would rather not dwell on, and on this first meeting, Gunning seemed particularly interested in it. He began cordially enough, but there was an atmosphere of threat that was very difficult to ignore.

'How are you finding Liverpool? I hope your lodgings are to your taste,' he began. I chose my words carefully and mentioned the attentiveness of the landlady. 'Good,' he said, leaning back in his chair as though to peruse me from a distance. 'It was the house of a man named Morgan; he was one of Mr Unsworth's associates,' he continued, and then after a pause, he added, 'By all accounts, this man betrayed my employer.'

He let this information hang in the air for a moment, before reaching for some papers on his desk. I hoped we would speak of Samuel Unsworth, but I was not quick enough to fill this brief gap in conversation with my questions. 'I have three testimonials here,' he said, laying them out in front of him like a stacked deck of cards. 'A favourable account of your studies in London, a promising future and so on; one from a senior surgeon from some Norfolk hospital; and another from a country doctor who you aided in various matters, including,' he paused to find the sentence in question, 'a particularly difficult lithotomy,' he read. 'What is a lithotomy?' I cleared my throat. 'It is the removal of a stone. In the instance you allude to, it was in the gentleman's bladder.' Gunning nodded as though he understood. 'Was it successful?' he asked. 'The doctor does not state the outcome.' I began to perspire at the memory of that dreadful day, but I can lie with equanimity when it is called upon. I told him it had been very successful, that the patient had made a full recovery.

The captain smiled and I relaxed slightly, but Gunning was far from finished. 'This last letter states that your employment ended in 1778 – four years ago,' he said. 'Where have you been for the last four years?' I had prepared for this exact eventuality. 'I cared for my father in his dwindling years. It was the least I could do.' I felt no remorse for this falsehood. In some ways, my father *is* dead. We have not seen each other for ten years. 'I see,' Gunning said, staring at me. 'Tell me, why have you sought employment on a slave ship, and why the *Othello*?'

My reasons were innumerable: my distaste for the trade but my need to bear witness, my ambition to do something useful and eventually contribute to its eradication, my failure as a general practitioner, my need for employment. I mentioned none of these motives to the captain, but instead told him what I thought he wanted to hear. 'I wish to travel,' I said, 'and Mr Unsworth's reputation is known even in Norfolk. I hear he is a good employer.' The captain grinned. 'Aye, that he is,' he said, 'if you do not cross him. He is also pitiless, and his contempt for the niggers is not to everyone's taste.' He watched me for a moment before continuing. 'Your role would be to see to the crew and select healthy slaves for transportation. Once they are selected, you must preserve them until we arrive in Jamaica.' I nodded and told him that I understood, but the captain was not convinced. 'I am not sure you do quite understand. Mr Unsworth will not tolerate the death of his slaves: you cannot work dead niggers. Each death will reduce profit, and that loss will be deducted from *your* salary.' The irony of keeping the slaves alive only for them to be worked to death did not escape me, but I kept my thoughts to himself. 'I will certainly endeavour to keep the Negroes alive,' I said, before adding, 'and as comfortable as possible during the voyage.' Gunning smirked at me, his features twisting grotesquely. 'Fuck their comfort. You must leave such absurd sensibilities behind. There is no place for them on a slave ship.' Gunning must have sensed my discomfort for he sighed and seemed to choose his next words carefully. 'Mr Unsworth is, as you said, a good employer. But he has become suspicious of late and does not trust even those who are most loyal to him,' he said, leaning forward and lowering his voice. 'He has installed one of his own men on the ship, a spy of sorts, a boy really, a half-nigger, a fly that'll squat in every part of the vessel and report back to Unsworth once we are on land.' He looked over my shoulder to check the door was still closed before continuing. '*He* will certainly not tolerate a waywardness of spirit or noble ideas about the slaves, and neither will I.'

I assured him that I understood, but the mention of another spy on board secretly perplexed me. I wanted to ask more but Gunning suddenly seemed to want rid of me; he handed me a bank note to purchase provisions for the voyage. He directed me to an apothecary on Fleet Street and wished me a good day. It was a strange first meeting, and I still think of it often whenever I have dealings with the captain. His character is not to my liking, but there was a hint of perception in that first encounter; I had the uneasy suspicion that he saw through my lies.

I soon became acquainted with members of the crew, with the first mate, a pleasant gentleman named Wyatt, and the second mate, a less gregarious man named Richards. I also met the carpenter, Parr, a cantankerous but humorous fellow. Gunning's mention of the 'spy' had intrigued me, and when I met the person in question, Heathcliff, I thought the captain's clear uneasiness had been unwarranted. But I underestimated the boy, for I believed his youth made him pliable. I was utterly mistaken in this, as I soon discovered in the long months between our delayed departure from Liverpool and our tumultuous arrival in West Africa.

After weeks of protraction and idleness, whilst the *Othello* remained sedentary in the Old Dock, fully rigged, her masts audibly groaning to be away, we finally boarded on September 14th and sailed with thirty crew and a cargo of silk, cotton, metal work and jewels, to use as currency upon our arrival in Sierra Leone.

I was eager to be gone, to begin my work, and the thought of my work, both as surgeon and spy, energised me. But the last three months at sea have been long and taxing. I had my books, and I attempted to learn Temne so that I could converse with the slaves in their own language, but I had failed to attune my body's rhythm to the sea's lilt; my seasickness was endless. I struggled to write the particulars of the voyage in this journal or to devote enough hours to studying, but I attempted to be convivial to the crew despite my natural reserve and antipathy. I ate dinner most evenings with Gunning, Wyatt and sometimes Heathcliff, and although I was initially loath to be in their company, I found the break in monotony beneficial, for the days were long and mostly uneventful, punctuated only with visits to my cabin. I set aside a few hours every day for a kind of clinic, but the men did not abide by these times, and I did not mind. There were boys with infected blisters on their palms, inexperienced sailors with seasickness, higher-ranking crewmen with stomach pains and diarrhoea, caused, I surmised, from the rich food they ingested. I was vigilant for scurvy; however, I saw no sign of it. These cases were not above my expertise and thus I began to feel at ease on the *Othello*. I had abandoned my past in England, and as far as the crew was concerned, I was a reputable and highly efficient doctor. Sierra

Leone still seemed an entire ocean away, and I did not yet dwell on the tasks I would have to perform there, until the day Heathcliff appeared at my cabin door.

Heathcliff was hardy from the outset and did not visit until the eighth week of our voyage. I had not attempted to converse at length with him in the weeks before his visit; for the captain had made it known that Heathcliff was Unsworth's man, and distrust and fear had spread through the ship like a sea mist. Heathcliff's reputation suited me, for while all eyes were on Unsworth's associate, I could retreat to my cabin and write this account without drawing any attention to myself.

This arrangement came to a sudden end with the arrival of Heathcliff.

I was initially at a loss, for he looked extremely well − young but physically strong, with no obvious pain or affliction. I asked him to sit down and enquired about his health. 'I am very well,' he said, smiling. 'How is your sickness?' This took me aback, for I was not aware my seasickness was widely known. 'It comes and goes now,' I said. 'It is no longer constant, but it is often worse at night when I have nothing to distract me.' I eyed Heathcliff. There was no tinge of sickness; he looked as well as the day we left Liverpool. 'Is it seasickness that ails you?' I asked, doubtfully. 'No,' he answered. 'My matter is of a non-medical nature.' I did not immediately respond, and I tried to appear nonchalant. If Heathcliff was not ill, then he was there on more serious business. I felt sweat blooming through my shirt, and I began to fuss with my collar before I could stop myself. Heathcliff seemed to take all this in.

'Do you know my purpose here, Doctor?' he asked, and before I could respond, Heathcliff continued. 'I am here for two reasons, one, to conduct all transactions in both Sierra Leone and in Mr Unsworth's plantation in Jamaica. A previous captain formed a contract with a smuggler, and my employer was betrayed. That smuggler is now rotting in the Tower and the captain of the vessel will never find a captaincy in England again. I am here to save Gunning from a similar fate.' I already knew all the particulars, but I did not interrupt him. 'The other reason is to do with the slaves. I am to run Mr Unsworth's interests in the West Indies after this voyage. I suppose I am his apprentice.' I raised my hand to interrupt. 'Please reach the matter you would like to discuss,' I said, growing more and more nervous the longer Heathcliff delayed. Heathcliff smiled at this, and said, 'This is the situation, Dr Avery, as I see it. I have attended to your conversations with the crew and the captain, and I do not think your heart is in the slave trade.' I know I paled at this, and then I laughed, too loudly, before motioning for Heathcliff to continue. 'Although there are similarities in our situations,' he said, ignoring my strange outburst, 'be sure, Doctor, that you and I differ when it comes to the niggers. But we are both spies in our varying ways. I am here to watch Gunning, and you are here to watch all of us, I think.' I kept my face expressionless and explained that I was there in the role of a surgeon only. 'Very well,' Heathcliff replied, 'then I am sure your journal is merely a logbook of ailments and cures, and you will not mind if I inspect it.'

I was stunned. How did he know about the journal? Heathcliff guessed my thoughts; it seems I am easy to read. 'I once kept a journal, Doctor,' he said, 'of the same cloth as yours.' I glanced at my desk, where the book was visible for anyone to take. I had been a fool. 'What do you propose?' I asked. 'Merely for us to keep out of each other's way, as much as possible on a vessel such as this. There is one other thing,' he said, standing slowly and filling the small cabin. 'My name is not to appear in your final report. I will have your word on this, Avery, unless you want our good captain to throw you overboard. There are murmurings of dissent in Liverpool, of the imminent end of this inhumane trade, as they call it, which would herald the end of Gunning. He would not take kindly to a nigger lover on his ship.' He spoke unnaturally, it seemed to me, as though he were using these words for the first time, but the threat behind them was practised, habitual, and symptomatic of a man accustomed to getting his own way.

Once alone, I took my journal and locked it in my medicine box. I would preserve my own life by 'keeping out' of Heathcliff's, but I will not omit him from my account, for if this abominable trade continues to flourish, then Heathcliff is its future.

January 18th

The days since my previous entry have been as full as the last hundred days at sea were empty. I have much to write, and until this evening, I admit to feeling too toil-worn to chronicle all I have experienced. We now have three hundred Negroes stored below. If I listen carefully, when the sea is calm, I hear their chains clinking. My cabin is directly above the ship's hold, a situation I was unaware of until recently.

How we came to acquire those Negroes, I will now recount in as detailed a manner as possible.

The captain's earlier prophecy, that all the hardy Negroes would be sold, proved accurate. He summoned me promptly the morning after we arrived; I was to accompany him ashore to appraise what was left of the slaves. I suspect he called on me early to avoid alerting Heathcliff of his plan. Gunning could, therefore, not conceal his disappointment and frustration when we found Heathcliff already on deck, and what followed between them was, to me, wholly unexpected.

'I was about to leave without you,' Heathcliff said, with devilry in his eyes. 'I have instructed Wyatt to take command, in our absence.' Gunning was suddenly sanguine with rage, implying, to my mind, that this was not the first time Heathcliff had deliberately gone over the captain's head, so to speak. I stepped back so as not to intrude, for I knew the captain could not ignore Heathcliff's encroachment with an audience present, therefore I turned away, pretending to be interested in something else.

The captain, after briefly glancing in my direction, moved to within a few inches of Heathcliff's face. 'I have to endure you, lad, I'm well aware of that,' he said. 'But none of my men answer to you, do you understand? Wyatt is *my* man.' Heathcliff did not flinch. Despite his youth, he was taller and broader than the captain. He looked his opponent in the eye and said, 'And *you* are *mine*.' This infuriated Gunning further. 'I've seen your kind before; you are not exceptional,' Gunning said, stepping away from Heathcliff. 'You watch and you scheme and you covet what is not yours. You're a half-nigger imposter from God-knows where. For all your fine words and your haughty bearing, that dirt from under your nails will always be there,' Gunning continued, seizing Heathcliff's hands; they were already larger than the captain's. 'See,' he said, as Heathcliff snatched them away from him. 'No matter how often you think you've scrubbed them clean, that dirt you were born in, were raised in, will never leave you.'

Heathcliff studied his fingernails carefully, lifting them up to his face. Gunning did not move. I glanced at my own fingernails, I could not resist, and then quickly placed my hands in my pockets. 'There is no dirt, Gunning,' Heathcliff said. 'But if there were, you are wrong to think that I would not willingly return to it. Not in my earliest form, that is true, but I will return and claim what is mine. Do you dare stand in my way?'

Gunning glared at him. 'You should have perished in the storm,' he said, spitting at Heathcliff's feet.

I had just resolved to escape to my cabin when Heathcliff launched himself at the captain. At less than half Gunning's age, Heathcliff is stronger than him and cares nothing of rank. He kicked the captain's legs from under him, and while the older man tried to get up, Heathcliff took a rope from the front mast and wound it around Gunning's neck like a noose. I watched, horror-stricken, and scanned the deck for other witnesses. The deck, at that time in the morning, was deserted.

'If you die, Captain,' Heathcliff said, his eyes aflame, 'I will tell Unsworth that you turned traitor, but if *I* die, well, you may as well stay in Jamaica, for you will be finished the moment you step onto the quayside in Liverpool.' Gunning tugged at the rope that was held fast around his throat.

I had to intervene, there was no-one else.

'Heathcliff, stop this madness,' I said, edging cautiously forward. 'For it is madness, I assure you.' Heathcliff looked up, as though seeing me for the first time. He had, I think, forgotten I was there. 'Let the captain go,' I said, reaching out to him with my hand, 'or this will not end well for you.' I touched his shoulder to root him in the present, and his eyes seemed to refocus, losing some of their ferocity.

'I do not wish you dead, Captain,' he said, shrugging my hand away and loosening the noose slightly. 'You are useful; you navigated us well through that storm. But I will finish you if you ever threaten me again. The men are not loyal to you or to anyone. There is a fortune to be made here; that is all that drives them.' He released the rope and Gunning fell forward clumsily, breathing hard. I moved to help him up, but he swatted my hand away, and slowly raised himself. His neck was flushed red. He stepped towards Heathcliff and glared at him. The youth did not baulk but stood tall. 'Well, Captain,' he said, smiling sardonically, 'at least we understand each other now.' Gunning did not verbally react but pushed past Heathcliff and led the way down the gangboard, still holding his throat.

The captain might have seemingly disregarded the event, but my nerves were wracked. I was shocked at the suddenness of the violence. My legs were shaking as I followed them, and more than once I very nearly toppled into the sea. My faculties were blunted, not merely from the shock of the event described above and how suddenly it was over for those involved, but the heat weighed on me like sin. I could feel the sun, not even fully risen yet, on the back of my neck, and I began to perspire freely, as I used to in my father's forge.

My father's forge, that place of sweat and fire, always repulsed me. I cannot think of my father's profession without shame. My brother, simpler and less studious than I was, grew to accept the clank of iron as inevitable, allowing me to hew my own way in the world. It is a cruel irony that despite escaping my father's legacy, I now found myself in a forge of a different kind.

I must have counted twelve furnaces on the quayside, but the African blacksmiths' business, the business of shackles and links, metal collars and iron muzzles, was of a different nature to my father and brother's trade. I record these 'instruments' here. I am uncertain how else to describe them, with nausea, for seeing those crude devices laid out on the floor was insubstantial when, not long afterwards, I witnessed them being used on those souls most deserving of our pity and used by Englishmen. Since arriving, I have watched sailors befriend the port's stray dog population, feeding and passing the time by teaching the animals tricks. Often, there are fights between rival strays, leaving at least one dog dead on the quay nearly every day, much to the sailors' grief. It seems the English would rather weep over a dead dog than preserve the life and freedom of a fellow-creature.

Gunning led us away from the quay and towards an outpost of clay huts and near empty cages. 'The best has already been taken, as I predicted,' Gunning said to no one in particular, turning away from the older and weaker slaves that remained. Although my legs were steadier, I could not dispel the sickness in my stomach, and with dread, I asked the captain what would happen to those that remained. 'They will be returned to the interior, or sent to work in the mines,' he said, staring intently at the huddle of thin and feeble bodies in the nearest cage. They were fly-coated and too wretched to shake them off. My stomach twisted as I watched one of the bloated insects crawl into an insensible woman's mouth.

'Do you not have the stomach for this work, Doctor?' Heathcliff asked suddenly. I pretended not to hear him and instead turned to the captain. 'I do not need to inspect them,' I said to Gunning, averting my eyes from the doomed slaves. 'I can see from this distance they are in terrible condition and would not survive the middle passage.' Gunning wiped perspiration from his forehead and loosened his collar. He appraised the slaves again. 'I agree,' he said eventually, before turning to Heathcliff. 'Are you of the same opinion?'

I tried to hide my surprise at this reversal in roles, but I don't think I hid my reaction well, for Gunning would not meet my eye. Heathcliff smiled and moved closer to the cage to appraise the potential cargo. He could count the ribs on the men, and the women, with their wilted breasts, were clearly too old. I hoped he would recognise these signs and not demand that I inspected the Negroes more closely. 'I am in agreement,' he said finally.

Without explaining his actions, the captain drew the attention of the African slave owner. He communicated with the Negro in broken Temne, an occurrence that amazed me; he had made no mention of his understanding of the language, despite knowing that I am striving to learn it. Heathcliff seemed less surprised than I. He listened attentively, watching the features and mannerisms of both men. He seemed to observe them both coolly, but he faced me when Gunning's back was turned and spoke quietly. 'Do you understand what is said between them?' I raised my hand and tilted it slightly, before whispering that I understood one or two words, the Temne word for slave and another word, which I thought meant price, but I now realise has a more precise meaning: *fcf mclc*, bargain.

The captain turned to us briefly, as did the slaver, who seemed interested in Heathcliff, owing to his darker complexion I assume, and then continued to converse with the slaver. I did not understand much of it, but still Heathcliff looked to me. I shook my head to indicate that I was unable to translate, and he glowered in response, baring his teeth, his dark eyes fierce, his act slipping for a moment, and then it passed, and he smiled at me. I was struck with how quickly he regained control, but I had seen enough that morning to realise him capable of extreme anger, even violence if thwarted. It was never the captain I should have been wary of.

The rest of the morning passed without incident, until midday, when the sun was so high that even the slavers seemed to admit defeat and went in search of shade. I hid in my cabin and attempted to find the translation of the key words from Gunning's conversation with the slaver. I was just beginning to settle into my task, when the first mate, Wyatt, appeared at my door to deliver a message from the captain. I was summoned to his cabin immediately. I tidied my papers, and followed Wyatt, who left me at the captain's door. When I entered, Heathcliff was already present, a fact Gunning seemed indifferent to. He informed me that a new stock of slaves had arrived from the interior, and they were temporarily held in barracoons in Lomboko. He urged me to ready myself, for we would depart for this place within the hour.

I imagine that going up the Gallinas River to Lomboko was like travelling back to the very beginnings of the world, when trees and plants and animals ruled, spreading, and pollenating and possessing every inch of the earth. Tortured mangroves, their roots writhing under the brown water, lined the muddy banks on both sides like a legion of cadavers. Alligators, half submerged in mud, sunned themselves on the clay shelves, and the flute-notes of unseen birds filled the thick air with foreboding.

The four oarsmen chosen from the crew silently cleaved through the water. The sound of drumming from concealed villages carried upriver and then faded.

It was a difficult journey, for neither Heathcliff nor the captain conversed with each other. Gunning seemed to tolerate him, after the events of that morning, but he sat morose with his jaw clenched. I sat between them and found no solace there or in the brilliance of the sun, for the back of my neck tingled under its glare and I craved shade when there was none.

Heathcliff sat, brooding. This new landscape of impenetrable forests pressed heavily on all of us, but particularly so on him. Wanting to relieve the tension and break the dense silence, I asked his opinion of the terrain. The loudness of my voice startled me and seemed to snap Heathcliff from his contemplation, for he blinked and stared at me as though I had injured him. He watched me for a moment before answering, as though weighing possible responses. The captain was listening, despite determinedly facing the opposite way. 'It is not to my liking,' he said finally. 'I like to see what is ahead of me,' and then after another pause, as though deciding what he could and could not reveal, he continued. 'I grew up in vast moorland, in Yorkshire, where you can see a storm brewing a mile away and know that it will rain in an hour, where you can see your enemy on the horizon and ready yourself. These trees are...terrible in their size,' he glanced at the captain and the oarsmen, and lowered his voice. 'I had a thought, Doctor, a moment ago, which unseated me, and my heart was like a boulder in my chest.' I leaned in closer, strangely transfixed by this new, pensive aspect to his character. 'I imagined,' he whispered, 'that this boat was a beetle, crawling at the foot of one of those immense trees, and that I was a speck on the back of that beetle.' I looked at him in wonder. 'You have just realised your own insignificance, Heathcliff,' I said quietly. 'Your place in the world. It is humbling and terrifying, is it not?' For a moment, I thought he was redeemable, that violence was not ingrained in him, but then he glanced at the others in the boat and smiled. 'You mis-understand me, Avery,' he said. 'I did wonder at my own nothingness when faced with these giants, that is true,' he pointed to the trees, 'but then I wondered how long it would take to destroy such a forest, to bring it under control. I don't think it would take long, with the correct instruments.'

I suddenly felt cold despite the heat, and I was about to enquire which 'instruments' he alluded to, when the captain uttered commands to the oarsmen, who veered the boat to the right and around a bend in the river. Heathcliff was alert as the river broadened, the trees fell back, and our view widened. The sense of oppression which had, in varying ways, probably affected each of us, lifted suddenly. The air was lighter, and the cries of birds now seemed far away.

Gunning pointed to where the water forked, where a single forested island was set within the river like an emerald. 'Lomboko?' I asked, again in a louder voice than I had intended. I was answered when a white fortress became visible above the trees, as pale as ivory, and the sounds of the forest were hushed by the shouts and cries of men.

Lomboko: I shudder at the word now, for it is a slave fortress, a slave factory, where thousands of souls pass through and thousands more perish. Its walls are sheer and dizzyingly high. The Spanish built it well, for no man could scale those walls, and when the gate shut behind us, I felt a desperate need to turn back. But I concealed this as best I could and allowed myself to be directed towards one of the barracoons. One of ten. The slaves were told to exit in single file and stand in a line. Their hands and feet were shackled, and they were all naked, both men and women. I knew what was expected of me, and proceeded to examine each slave, whilst under the watchful gaze of both Gunning and Heathcliff.

Gunning was in a capricious mood, and invited Heathcliff, as a 'novice slaver' to instruct me on the best way to examine the slaves. Heathcliff did not shy away from this task, and he warmed to it very quickly. He had me begin at each slave's head before working my way down. I checked their eyes, their teeth, the men's stomachs, and the women's breasts; I pressed their outer and inner thighs, and inspected the men's testicles and the women's vulvas, as a way of ascertaining any venereal disease. I did my utmost to be gentle, but the women wept. I inspected over four hundred slaves over the course of the afternoon, until I was exhausted and near weeping at my task, but I steadied myself and thought of the greater good, that my work here might save thousands from the same fate. Thus, feigning nonchalance, I selected three hundred of the healthiest Negroes, who were then taken to be shaven, and Heathcliff agreed their transportation to the harbour the following morning, in exchange for the entirety of our cargo. Captain Gunning's only use during this transaction was his knowledge of the language, thus he regained an element of control in the proceedings, however paltry.

'You have your three hundred, Captain,' I said, submerging my hands in a trough of water meant for the stray dogs. I tried to wash the day away, but my hands were stained with the men and women I had just condemned. 'You've done well today, John,' the captain said. He had never before used my Christian name. 'I'll make sure to mention that in my correspondence to Mr Unsworth,' he said, and addressing Heathcliff, he continued, 'or perhaps it is *your* place to inform him.' Heathcliff grinned at the captain. 'I'm certain he would expect correspondence from both of us, Captain, now we are on land,' he said.

I dried my hands on my tunic and turned away from them; I was too tired to attend to their rivalry. 'Where are you going?' the captain asked, as he and Heathcliff prepared to finalise the transaction. I was heading back to the boat, but I was far enough away from the captain to feign deafness. The sun had arced across the sky in the time I had been selecting slaves for transportation. There was a red tinge above the treetops and the day had cooled. When I reached the boat, I lay down and tried to sleep, despite the flies that settled on me and the murmurings of the oarsmen.

I do not remember much of the journey back to the *Othello*. I only remember ascending the ship and making straight for my cabin, where I expected to sleep instantly, but each time I closed my eyes I was back in that slave fortress, where the women wept when I touched them. It was all too much to bear. I made myself a tincture of laudanum and within moments I slept the deep, dreamless sleep of a person without guilt.

When I awoke, some twelve hours later, preparations were underway for the arrival of the slaves. I was dazed after the laudanum, but I had slept so well that it was a worthy price to pay.

Whilst I had slumbered, the sailors had emptied the hold and transferred the cargo to crates and stores on the quayside, in readiness for the exchange. Once I was dressed, I approached Wyatt and asked when we could expect the new cargo. He intimated it would be within the hour, since slaves from Lomboko would be made to walk through the night, which in a way was a kindness, he said, since they would not be subjected to the 'infernal African sun'.

By noon, the slaves had arrived. They were marched on board in gangs of ten, but they were then freed and instantly stowed below; the women and men were separated by a partition wall, erected by the ship's carpenter. They would remain below until we were clear of the coast, for Negroes, as Gunning informed me, become so land-sick they 'have the propensity to jump overboard'. One or two of the younger men were visibly distraught, crying out in fear and pointing to the harbour. I discovered later, from Heathcliff, that the Africans had so little understanding of their fates that they believed they were doomed to be eaten by the crew – a childish horror that I found very interesting. It seems our notion of barbarism is identical; cannibalism is a human revulsion, regardless of place of birth or caste. We share a humanity with the Negroes, a fact that must be powerfully expressed when the trials begin.

Once below, panic began to take hold. Each slave was manacled to chains that hung from the ceiling. I was reminded of a slaughter-house, an image I knew would be intensified as the conditions inevitably worsened during the middle passage. Due to the number of slaves, the ceiling height was reduced to 22 inches, to accommodate another floor above the lower hold. I could not comprehend how any human could breathe in such a menial space, and I voiced my concern to the captain, who explained they would be permitted on deck twice a day once we were clear of land. This did little to comfort me, since the height did not permit the Negroes to sit. Instead, the sailors, brandishing the cat, urged them to lie down in spoon fashion on the boards, which they did, despite their alarm. The captain explained in Temne to the slaves that they must always return to this position when bidden. My Temne is rudimentary, but I have a little understanding, although hearing it spoken is very different to learning the language from books. The Negroes were silent as Gunning spoke, making no indication that they understood him.

I returned to the deck to inspect the hatches and found Heathcliff undertaking the same task. The hatches on this ship are grated, and the carpenter, for air to circulate more easily, has cut out an additional number, but it is insufficient to keep the captives cool, particularly those underneath this level.

Heathcliff was watching as the bodies below writhed like snakes, attempting to make themselves as comfortable as their humiliating positions could afford. I greeted him with a wary civility, for after his violence with the captain, I was a little afraid of him.

'They are more fortunate than some, Doctor,' he said, in response to my expression, I imagine. I find my 'mask' slipping more often recently. 'And how would you enjoy such conditions, Heathcliff?' I asked, my voice breaking slightly, which I could not conceal. 'I would despise it,' he answered. 'It is not my fate to be penned like a pig to the slaughter, but I have suffered cruelties and indignities, do not doubt that.' I averted my eyes from Heathcliff, and asked, 'Is any man meant for such a fate?'

He smiled. 'The niggers are accustomed to this life.' He paused with mischief in his eyes. I was certain he was baiting me. 'Slavery is their choice, Doctor. I would destroy this ship plank by plank if I were in their position, but they do nothing except make themselves more comfortable,' he pointed to the bodies below, now still. 'They accept their lot and there is a relief, is there not, in knowing that you are exactly where you should be? Who are we to deprive them of that certainty?' My attention was now all on Heathcliff. 'That is an interesting viewpoint,' I said. 'But some would argue that the slaves are human beings, no different from you or me.' I studied my opponent and considered asking about his parentage, for Heathcliff may have European features, but his colouring, particularly his black eyes, allude to a more obscure ancestry. 'Yes, they are men,' Heathcliff said. 'But not all men are cut from the same cloth, which is a point I am sure you agree with.' I nodded, conceding the point. 'Yes, but to continue the metaphor, some men are handed richer cloth than others. Until society treats all men with fairness, there can be no equality.' I had not expected to engage in debate, and my mind felt heavy after the laudanum. 'Any man can improve his circumstances,' Heathcliff responded, smiling. 'Any man with a strong will and a sense of injustice can choose to discard the hand given to them and fashion a new future for himself. Which brings me back to my point about *them*,' he said, nodding towards the slaves below. 'There is no strength of will there. Merely acceptance, and acceptance, in my mind, is a choice.'

I paused for a minute to order my thoughts, watching the slaves' futile efforts to find comfort, and feeling a profound sympathy with their plight. 'Some would argue,' I eventually said carefully, 'that occasionally a man's choice is made for him, and when the weight of history is behind that choice, it takes the might of many to instigate change for individuals such as those stored beneath our feet.' I tried to utter this point gently, for Heathcliff had not spoken at length about slavery to me for many weeks, and although I distrust the boy, I knew it was a subject he felt, and still feels, very strongly about.

'Very well, I have a question, if you would answer it,' Heathcliff said. I hesitated, I had my own question for Heathcliff but, as often happens, I had missed the opportunity to ask it. 'What would you ask?' I said quietly. 'Only this – what is your heritage? Is your father a medical man?' I was taken aback by his bluntness, which seemed so out of keeping with his approach thus far. I do not speak of my father to many, of my low birth and self-improvement, and I would not allow it to be used as evidence to justify the belief that the weak deserve to be enslaved by the strong. 'Yes,' I lied. 'I am very fortunate in my parentage.'

I made my excuses to Heathcliff, and feeling rather unsettled by our dispute, I returned to my cabin in an agitated state. I mixed a little opium from my medicine cabinet with water, and within a minute, I began to feel calmer, and I sank into a deep sleep.

When I awoke, many hours later, in darkness, with the events of the last few days ever present despite my peaceful slumber, I lit a candle and commenced this journal entry. Committing the recent events to paper has unburdened me, and I begin to wonder if this journal serves two purposes: to provide evidence for the destruction of this abhorrent trade; and as a form of curation, a physic for the suffering I must witness.

It is now near morning, the sky is reddening, I have been writing for half the night, and I must rest. We set sail for Jamaica on tomorrow's tide.

February 25th

The month since we set sail from Sierra Leone has been arduous, and I begin to doubt my ability to perform my duties, as both surgeon and chronicler.

The daily routine of life on a slave ship, punctuated with small skirmishes and acts of barbarity, is beginning to prove more of a challenge than the inertia of the journey from Liverpool, and I do not feel my usual self; although, arguably, a sense of self must be jeopardized when a person is pushed to the limits of their forbearance, therefore perhaps it is a price I should expect to pay. But if my compass is to go awry, I merely ask that one day, when this is over, I will point North once again.

The middle passage, as it is called, spans the Atlantic, and this is the third week devoid from land of any description. The slaves wailed below for eight days, for although they could not see the disappearing shore of Sierra Leone, I think they must have sensed the separation. Many wanted to die. They could not jump into the sea, for they were not yet allowed on deck, therefore they refused to eat. The captain found the strongest rebel, and while Wyatt administered the cat, I was tasked with pushing a pipe down the Negro's throat through which liquid rice could be forced into his stomach. The pain from the cat made him unable to protest and hindered any attempt to eject the pipe. This spectacle was carried out in front of the other slaves, and it had the desired effect, for the attempts at suicide through starvation ceased. The captain describes such acts as 'forcible cruelties that cannot be avoided'. I suspect that he begins to see my distaste for the work and seeks to justify such actions as a necessary evil, that no man on board would find enjoyment in inflicting pain on the slaves. I disagree. I think cruelty becomes some men more than others.

Wyatt can administer the cat until the Negro's back is the bark of a tree and his own face and garments are spotted with the man's blood, and yet he speaks with gentleness and has shown kindness to the inexperienced sailors and boys. The carpenter, who transformed this vessel into a moving prison, makes merry and speaks with affection of his wife, Margery. They have split their being and can therefore sleep soundly. Captain Gunning is hardened and feels nothing for his cargo, and this antipathy allows him to also sleep soundly. I cannot sleep soundly. The position of my cabin, directly above the hold, preys on my mind, particularly at night; I have begun to ration my store of opium, for I fear I will run out before the slaves are delivered, and my nights will once again become long and filled with the cries from below. Heathcliff, who I begin to comprehend finally, and who has, I think, singled me out, be it for good or ill, confessed his own sleeplessness to me during week two of the crossing.

We had not conversed at length since our disagreement about the nature of slavery, and his astonishing question about my parentage. I was regularly in his company during dinner, and he was often present if I was called to inspect the health of a slave, but I avoided being alone in his presence. He spent a great deal of time viewing the slaves through the hatches, a vision that must have unnerved the Negroes: the blackness of his silhouette against the bright sky. The captain tolerated him, simply because he had no other choice, but the rest of the crew were quite vocal about his strange behaviour.

When he came to my cabin, after two weeks of avoiding each other's company, he sat and began to unburden himself. I informed him that I am not a priest, that if he wished to confess, he would be better to voice his transgressions to the waves. I turned to my books to signal the end of our conversation, but he did not move from the seat. Instead, he seemed to settle there. I could not account for this, thus I waited for him to speak, feeling very uncomfortable. I found myself inadvertently glancing at my medicine box.

'Do not concern yourself, Doctor. I am not here to disturb you. I will leave you to your Lady Laudanum very soon.' Shocked, I replied that I had no conception of what he meant. This seemed to anger him, and he snapped. 'Come, Doctor, I tire of this. I recognise an opium addiction when I see one, and it will not be long before Gunning and the other men recognise your pallor and infernal nervousness for what they are.' The room blurred at his words, and I felt a terrible sickness come over me. I closed my eyes temporarily and breathed deeply. When I opened them, Heathcliff was still there, of course, but my heart had ceased its maddening tattoo, and I could think more clearly. 'I find it difficult to sleep, Heathcliff, and the effect of sleep deprivation on the brain and consequently on the body, can be catastrophic.' Heathcliff's answer surprised me. 'Yes, indeed. This brings me to why I have visited you today. Sleep, Doctor, is a bitch, for she deprives me of rest only to plague me with nightmares when I finally overcome her.' I was surprised, and wondered if he had changed his view on the trade he was to be the champion of. 'I have not,' he said with disdain. 'I do not dream about *them*. I dream about somewhere else, a house on the moors. The moors would be flowering at this time of year, but in my dream the heather is black, and the birds are all dead. There is a hand smashing through a lattice, a hand that I hold and will not release, despite the horror of its owner, ordering me to release her.'

He had spoken briefly about his past on one or two occasions that I have not recounted here, of his regard for a girl from his past. 'Is it the girl you have spoken of who comes to you through the window?' I asked. He nodded, his face softening. 'Cathy,' he said. 'Her name is Cathy.' I edged nearer to him. 'I have no-one at home,' I said. 'You are very fortunate.' But any degree of sympathy seems to have the opposite effect on Heathcliff as it would on most; it made him recoil. 'I dream of distant ghosts, far away from here, ghosts that I long to return to. But these are the slut Sleep's tricks, and I will have no more of them. I will not take your Lady, but if you have a draught that will not alter my mind or my will, then I would gladly receive it, Doctor.'

I opened the medicine box with the key that I always keep on my person and searched for the valerian roots I had procured before setting sail from Liverpool. I had only purchased three roots, and I gave the smaller one to Heathcliff. 'This is the root of a plant that sedates and relaxes. Grind no more than a finger of it into a cup of hot water and drink it an hour before you retire. You have enough for seven nights,' I said, handing it to him. 'It is not always effective, particularly if your body is accustomed to stronger sedatives or opiates, but I do not think that is the case in this instance.'

He rose to leave, but something came over me – a desperation to escape the present, to unburden myself to a person instead of merely these pages – therefore I called him back. 'Do not wish those dreams of elsewhere away, Heathcliff,' I said. 'For I would do anything to live in them.'

He frowned and then smirked at my sentiment, his dreams of a lost love forgotten. He spoke harshly. 'We will reach Jamaica in ten weeks, and then within three months, we will set sail again as wealthier men. You must bear it the best you can; or if you cannot, *voice your fears to the waves*, Doctor, and if the waves answer, then I suggest you join them. Leave your accursed books and journals to me, for I would happily drown them on your behalf once you are gone.'

This evening, when I slip into deep slumber, this journal will be locked in my medicine cabinet, and I will sleep holding the key to my heart like a talisman.

March 16th

We are four weeks from the coast of Jamaica, if we are not tempest-tossed and delayed, and my store of opium has diminished considerably. I fear to think how I will manage without it.

Five days ago, I amputated a boy's leg at the knee, and three nights ago he died. I used a considerable amount of opium to ease his suffering, all the while selfishly wondering if he needed it as much as I did. I cannot think of my behaviour without abhorrence. Wyatt could not bear the boy's agony and reprimanded me for callousness. I had no other choice but to administer nearly all my remaining opium.

The boy, Henry, was no more than twelve years old. He was sprightly and performed his duties with diligence. Wyatt favoured him and always set him above the other boys, therefore I can see how the boy's suffering must have affected Wyatt and I do not blame him for his subsequent animosity towards me. I have performed my duties poorly and the rest of the crew knows of my carelessness. I am shunned by all except Heathcliff.

The boy, Henry, came to me with a deep cut on his left leg two weeks before I carried out the amputation. He had injured it on an old rivet and the wound was infected. I admonished him for not coming to me sooner, for the boy was now feverish and the skin surrounding the injury was mottled and flame hot to the touch. There was no odour then, thus I did not think all was lost for the boy. I gave him mercury to lower his fever and a salve to administer on the injury. I sent him back to the deck and thought no more of him, for I had made a discovery amongst the female slaves that worried me considerably.

I am not sure how I neglected to discover it in Sierra Leone, but one of the slaves is pregnant. There are a hundred women on board, and I can only assume that the tensions of that awful day, combined with the exhausting task of inspecting over four hundred Africans, affected the diligence of my work, for she is, I think, nearly eight months with child.

The conditions in the hold are desperate, there is no room to stretch or stand up, thus I requested that the woman in question be given more comfortable accommodation. The captain laughed at this suggestion, and asked me, 'Where do you propose to place her, doctor?' When I did not immediately respond, for I had not considered the practicalities of the request, he continued, 'Give up your own cabin if you wish and sleep in the hold with the slaves. I'm sure they would be most accommodating.' When I did not reply, Gunning looked at me curiously, 'Or perhaps you would *like* to install her in your cabin,' he said with a half-smile. 'I do not know what you mean,' I stated plainly. 'Well,' he said, shrugging, 'you wouldn't be the first to satisfy your urges – we're far from civilisation, Avery.' I was horrified when I understood his implication and assured him that I merely had immense sympathy for the woman's plight.

It was a week after this conversation that I amputated the boy's leg. Wyatt assisted me throughout the surgery. The boy was skin and bone, but his leg still proved difficult to sever. I sweated profusely, as I am now, reliving this terrible, terrible ordeal. The boy's screams shattered my nerves and silenced the slaves below.

When Gunning appeared, I asked him, as calmly as I could, to assist by holding the boy still. 'Henry,' Wyatt said. 'Henry, listen to me. This will be over soon, but you must stay still.' I was grateful for Wyatt then, for I could not find it within me to comfort the boy. I continued to saw, and the boy continued to scream. An operation that can and should be done in two minutes took nearly ten. My hands trembled throughout, and what remained of his leg, to my horror, would not have looked amiss in a slaughtery. Wyatt's anger had been building gradually, but I was still shocked by how suddenly it peaked. 'Damn you, Avery,' he said, visibly trembling with rage. 'A fucking butcher would have made better work of it. If this boy dies, you are responsible, do you hear?' I glanced at the boy and then looked at the bloody pulp of his leg and vomited onto my boots.

The captain regarded me with disgust, but then the boy began to cry, and Gunning's attention was drawn away for a moment. When he refocused on me, he spoke urgently and forcefully. 'Fetch pain relief, Avery,' he ordered. I must have hesitated too long, for the captain reached for my collar and pushed me out of the door and into the passageway. 'Fetch the opium,' he said, his eyes wild. 'Or I shall throw you overboard. You are an abomination to your profession.'

Chastised and still weak from the amputation, I stumbled to my cabin with the boy's cries echoing in every corner of the ship. I gathered most of my opium store, reeling with fear and dread of the weeks to follow, and returned to Gunning. He was still in the passageway, pacing. When he saw me, he opened the door and pushed me inside.

The boy's face was waxen, and he still moaned without end. Wyatt had removed his belt and used it as a tourniquet. It only then occurred to me how little control I had of my faculties; I had left the boy to bleed to death. Without meeting his eye, I asked Wyatt to tighten the tourniquet, as I administered the opium. 'Stitch the wound,' he commanded, his bile clearly rising again. 'No,' I said quickly, for I did not trust myself to complete the surgery, and the boy had suffered enough. 'It will heal by granulation,' I explained, although I have only seen it in abdominal wounds. 'A scab will form quickly, as long as we can keep the area clean.'

Wyatt, I'm afraid, saw the flaw in my approach, and looked expressly at the captain. But before they could admonish me, the boy's moans had become screams again. I had given him enough opium to numb the pain, but that was not what ailed him. He had seen his amputated leg, which I had left on the floor – a mangled, dead thing – and the horror of seeing it separate from his body had overcome him. 'Get *that* the fuck out of here!' Gunning shouted.

I picked up the leg and staggered back into the passageway. I tucked it, still bleeding, under my arm and climbed the ladder up to the deck, where I came upon Heathcliff. 'What the devil…' Heathcliff could not finish his sentence, but merely stared at me, shocked. In the glare of the sun, I realised I was smeared in blood. Heathcliff was struck into silence at the sight of me. I pushed past him and quickly threw the leg overboard. I watched it bob vertically for a moment, before sinking to the depths.

'Why did you not remove the shoe?' Heathcliff asked, appearing beside me. I had not even considered the shoe. 'There was no time,' I said, for it seemed plausible. 'Will he live?' he asked, scrutinising me. I knew he had not heard of the calamitous operation, not yet, and I wanted to savour the few moments remaining before the crew discovered my ineptitude. 'I hope so,' I said. 'He came to me over a week ago; the wound was not gangrenous then, therefore I thought he had a fair chance of fighting the infection.' Heathcliff nodded. 'The boy is well-liked,' he said. 'I hope for your sake he survives.'

We both looked out to sea, in all its unfathomable emptiness. I have seen sea birds on this voyage, even an albatross once, but marine life is scarce. There were shoals of unidentifiable fish near the coast of Africa, but that could have been a lifetime ago. Considering this conversation now, I recognise that I had suffered some disturbance of the mind following the amputation, for I cannot otherwise account for my next words. 'Perhaps the leg will attract a shark,' I said, unwisely speaking my bewildered thoughts aloud. 'I have always wanted to see a shark.'

Heathcliff seemed to stare at me for an age. 'Perhaps you should return to the boy,' he said, and when I walked back towards the ladder, he added, 'or perhaps you would prefer to return to that pregnant whore in the hold.' I did not have the faculties to manage Heathcliff's moods that day – he was, and is, like a pendulum, swinging from friend to foe in a matter of moments. 'You care more for the unborn whelp of a slave than a boy of your own colour,' he called after me.

I decided then, and it was a rash decision, to bite back and voice my thoughts on Heathcliff's parentage. What, I thought, did I have to lose? 'And you,' I said, turning to look at him, 'care more for a boy of my colour than a desperate woman of your hue. It seems we have a paradox, Heathcliff.' I turned back to the ladder, and as I prepared to descend, Heathcliff began to laugh. It was a cold, ill-meaning outburst, and I knew then I had made a mistake in responding to his insult.

The boy died later that evening, and I was not on deck when he was committed to the sea, which I now accept was foolish of me, for my absence was undoubtedly noted. I hid away in my cabin, measuring out my remaining opium store. I took a small vial of laudanum, and it was enough to provide the relief that I craved and needed.

I emerged the next day and determined to attend dinner, hoping that with time to consider, the crew had become sympathetic to my situation, but the ill-feeling was palpable when I entered the dining room and I instantly regretted leaving my cabin. Heathcliff began the attack, which I had expected after our last conversation, but I was still not prepared for his cruelty or his persistence. 'How are you sleeping, Doctor?' he asked first. The others remained silent. 'How is your hand? Is it steady?' he persisted. I glanced at Gunning for support, who looked away, and at Wyatt, who stared back at me with hatred. 'Did you throw your saw in the sea, blunt and bloodstained as it was?' Heathcliff asked. 'And your near-empty medicine store, how will you manage?'

The cook brought in the first course, and I glanced at him with some relief, but he threw my bowl in front of me and much of the soup spilled onto the table. I began to understand the depths of the crew's animosity, and I had an overwhelming urge to weep.

Heathcliff continued to press, to push me to the edge of my forbearance. 'Is a surgeon still a surgeon if he kills his patients?' he asked, leaning towards me. The captain dropped his spoon, and the clang drew everyone's attention. 'You should finish your meal in your cabin, Avery,' he said, gesturing to the door.

'I am very sorry about the boy,' I began. 'Damn you, his name was Henry Stephenson,' Wyatt interjected coldly. 'Amputations are never simple, and if the ... Henry had come to me sooner, I could have treated the wound successfully,' I tried to explain, addressing Wyatt. 'I think that is enough from you, Avery,' Gunning said, rising. 'Take your bowl and retire to your cabin.'

All my energies must now be spent on the slaves, more as a distraction than diligence on my behalf, for I find the hostility of my peers difficult to bear. I want the voyage over so that I can submit my findings and be done with it, but I am not certain how I will fare on the return voyage with the crew so set against me.

March 21st

My store of opium is now empty, and I must face what is to come.

My hand shakes as I write this, for the night demons that I have thus far chased away, will now crowd darkly around my bed. There is to be no escape this time.

I have seen the effects of opium removal, and I am aware of what lies ahead of me: the sweating, the chills. The visions. I will want to die a hundred times before it is ended, and only a locked door will save me. I have given the key to Heathcliff since he is the only person on board with full intelligence of my situation. I wonder at my judgment, and whether I will regret this action, but there is no other person to ask, no other person who would agree to such an undertaking. He is to be my gaoler, be it for good or ill.

I have sufficient water for three days captivity but only a small provision of food, since I will be unable to eat. I have procured three more chamber pots. I hope that number shall be sufficient.

When I write again it will be with a steady hand, God willing.

March 26th

My three days of penance were prolonged to five days, for despite my instruction, Heathcliff did not open the door until then.

He claimed the ship had been in the throes of an awful storm and the captain wanted all men on deck, apart from me, it would seem, and as a result he was unable to release me at the agreed time. I thought I had been lucid for nearly two days, and I had no recollection of a storm. 'But nothing looks amiss here,' I pointed out, turning my head as far as I could from my position on the bed. My body ached terribly, and it was with some effort that I managed to scan the cabin for breakages. 'Your senses are still adrift,' Heathcliff said, before turning to my desk and casually pulling my medicine box and my papers off the edge of the table. The box, which I always keep locked, did not open but the thud as it hit the floorboards worried me. 'See?' Heathcliff said, wide-eyed with feigned innocence. 'You did not even perceive that your prized medicine box had fallen in the storm.'

I was weak with hunger and could not prevent Heathcliff from destroying my cabin. He strewed my clothes on the bed and pushed my chair to the floor. I watched helplessly as he kicked over one of the chamber pots. I retched at the stink, but Heathcliff seemed unmoved by it. 'This is madness,' I said. 'Have you lost your senses?' He edged away from the urine pooling at his feet. 'I am merely making a point,' he said. 'There was a storm. The ship was nearly destroyed.'

I knew better than to argue with him. I still needed him – a fact that appalled me. 'Where is the captain?' I asked, as I slowly and painfully sat up in bed. The cabin was spinning, but I had to focus. 'Did he enquire about my absence?' I managed to ask.

'He did,' Heathcliff said. 'I told him you were dead or very soon would be. It was the first time any of my utterances inspired pleasure in him.'

Heathcliff leaned against the furthest wall from the bed and appraised me. If my face was as mottled and grey as my hands, then I could guess at his thoughts. 'Am I transformed?' I asked. 'I think I have aged these last few days.' Heathcliff nodded slowly. 'You have looked better,' he said simply. 'Gunning will be surprised to see you at dinner,' he said, still scrutinising me. 'He will take you for a ghost.'

I sensed that Heathcliff's mood had altered since his wilful destruction of my cabin, for he stepped closer to me and spoke quietly. 'I was once locked away for weeks and left for dead,' he said. 'I will send someone to clear this mess. I will be back shortly with bread and water.'

I watched him leave the room and then I lay down when I was certain he had not locked the door. I was exhausted, and increasingly perplexed by Heathcliff's strange conduct. I had read of dual personality disorders as a medical student, but I had never encountered a potential sufferer until now. I do not have the credentials or the experience to diagnose the affliction, for I am beginning to accept my own limitations, but there are two opposing forces in Heathcliff, of *that* I am certain.

I had only closed my eyes for moments when a young seaman arrived to clean my cabin. He brought a mop for the floor and took my other chamber pots away. Heathcliff returned as promised. He watched me eat the bread and then left. I accept that I will never know his motives, but I begin to grow strong again, although I fear I will never be what I once was.

April 2nd

Upon my return to life on board, not a soul remarked or enquired of my absence. The captain did, however, announce that I was 'returned', which I found an odd phrasing. Before I could respond, he turned and beckoned me to follow him. I struggled to keep pace with him, but I noticed, as we moved from the deck to the hold, that no-one, not even the cook or the carpenter, acknowledged my existence. I am a ghost, it would seem, and I have begun to feel immaterial, wraithlike.

'You may return to your duties,' Gunning said, stopping suddenly. 'But you will not, under any circumstances, speak with First Mate Wyatt. Stay out of his way, for no man will come to your aid if there is a quarrel between you.'

I noticed that my throat felt dry, and I became aware of a throbbing in my head, as my body continued to adjust to life without the opium. There was also a new sensation, a lurch in my stomach and a feeling of drifting. I was afraid, but after a moment, I managed to regain a degree of focus. 'How are the slaves? How is the pregnant woman?' I asked. 'She is taking the space of two, and the other women hiss at her and strike her.' I was horrified. 'Are they not comforting her?' It was not Gunning but Heathcliff that answered. I was struck by how suddenly he appeared, or perhaps my senses were still dulled. 'I have found,' Heathcliff said, 'that the tyrant can ground down his slaves, but they do not turn against him. Instead, they in turn crush those beneath them.' I shook my head. 'That is an obscene theory,' I said. 'Not at all,' he answered, with no conflict or uncertainty. 'They will not tolerate another mouth down there, I assure you.' He asserted his opinion with the authority of a captain. The world has tilted since my convalescence; I am adrift when those around me have become sure-footed. I fear that Heathcliff is now fully-formed.

I obeyed Gunning's order to examine the female slaves, although I had a deep dread of it. I remember thinking I would need to be observant, since I have not written a detailed account of this trade for many days, but I am undone, and I now find myself unable to accurately report on the conditions in the hold. I am an even worse spy than I am surgeon, for I cannot remember what I saw. I informed the second mate that the child would be born soon, perhaps within the week, yet I cannot recall how I came by this intelligence. When I close my eyes, I cannot 'see' the woman, a worrying development that again I cannot account for, since my visual memory has always been of the first order.

I shall endeavour again to sleep tonight. Sleep is a balm for most afflictions, from chronic pain to hurt minds, therefore I pray that I am successful; I begin to feel the slipping of my spirit, if there is such a thing. I need a deity, but if there is a God, he has turned away from the *Othello*. He does not look upon us, for all the devils are here.

April 12th

I must speak of horrors, although I do not have the words nor the stomach for it. The tremors, which had ceased for a time, have returned, and my hand is unsteady as I write this, but write it I must.

The baby was born at just after one o'clock this afternoon. It was pushed into the world in a ball of blood and mucus, and with no knowledge of the bondage that awaited it. I caught the child, cleared its airway, cut the cord, and tried to tell the mother in Temne that it was a boy. The woman snatched the baby from me and guided it to her breast. The other women kept their distance, their intentions as inscrutable as night. I thought of Heathcliff's odious supposition and hoped the women were wary of me rather than the woman and her baby. I waited for the placenta, and once it was safely delivered, I placed it in a bucket with the towels I had used and returned to the deck with the intention of throwing the afterbirth into the sea. But once on deck, the brightness of the sun splintered in my eyes, and I could not see except in tiny shards. It was like seeing the world in a broken mirror.

I placed the bucket down and stared at its contents. I knew it was a placenta. Logic demanded that it was a placenta. I tried to blink the image away, but the thing was seemingly still in the bucket: a monstrous pulsing jellyfish. I had the urge to find a stick and jab at it, a boy again, unaware of his own cruelty.

I looked away and stepped over the mass, fearful that the tendrils of my mind would wind themselves around my ankles. I checked my legs once I was clear of the bucket, and said, 'It's a placenta. Only a placenta,' to no-one. But the jellyfish remained with me. It was a throbbing fleck in the corner of my eye, a feeling of dread in my stomach, it was there in the rapid beats of my heart. My vision began to restore, although I was now sceptical of my own reality, and I noticed others on deck: they stood in clots and I had the distinct feeling that I was being discussed, and not favourably.

When I first heard the screams, I did not immediately react or realise this was the true reason so many were on deck. A slave ship is full of noises, from wailing to tribal singing, from the creaking masts to the trilling waves. But I realised as I listened that I had never heard such roaring before in my life.

The sun was still blinding, and my vision is prone to betraying me, thus I did not immediately comprehend what I was witnessing.

The woman I had tended not half an hour hence was being dragged by two sailors back into the hold. I remember wondering why she was on deck. Her belly was an empty sack and her inner thighs glistened with blood; she should have been resting. It was at this moment that I realised the screams were emanating from her. She bit and scratched her captors, until she saw me. She called out, her eyes pleading. I could not react. I did nothing to help her. Even when I saw Heathcliff and I fully comprehended the scene in front of me, I did nothing. My powerlessness when faced with a cruelty I had hoped to end was too much for me to bear.

Heathcliff took the baby from Wyatt and perused its face. He held the infant aloft in the manner of baptism. Gunning turned away, but I watched in horror as Heathcliff, still holding the squawking child, its head lolling on its neck, dropped it into the sea.

It made no sound as it hit the water, and no man spoke. There was only the howling from below.

It was the sound of a heart rupturing.

Samuel Unsworth

Liverpool

February – August 1783

'Sir, I wish to return to Speke.'

It had been a strained breakfast, and I expected an entreaty of some sort, but not this. Henrietta is thoughtless and ignorant like most girls; I had expected a request for an increase in allowance or a frivolous demand for an exotic pet from the colonies; I anticipated stepping in monkey shit for the foreseeable future. But a return to Speke? I had not anticipated that.

Speke: the very word is more than I can bear. I named my plantation in Jamaica New Speke, but that was before Emma died. Now the word summons images of a putrid sick bed, her prolonged, visible suffering, my reliance on satisfying my urges even as Emma drew her last breath. The very presence of those cravings at such a time seemed unnatural even to me. I beat Hana as punishment for my lust for her, and I did not visit her again until after Emma's funeral. It was, after all, the very least I could do.

'Sir, did you hear me?' Henrietta asked, drawing me from my thoughts.

'You wish to return to Speke,' I said.

'Yes, I miss the countryside and the peace,' she said, looking at me with her mother's eyes. They were dulled like Emma's were in her final weeks.

I finished my tea and forced myself to meet those eyes. 'Henrietta, please correct me if I am mistaken, but you loathe Speke,' I said. 'Is 'loathe' too strong a word?' I did not give her time to answer. 'Your sister petitioned me to 'release' you. She said you were growing wild with dullness. Are you under the impression that Speke has been magically transformed like in one of those books you read? Have your fairies been hard at work?'

She stiffened at this. 'I am not a child. Not anymore.'

'And so, you have put away childish things, is that it?'

'I wish to return to Speke.'

'Repeating the request does not make it more valid, Henrietta,' I said.

She had spent the previous six months in near solitude. I had employed the services of the most esteemed doctors in Liverpool and attempted to be patient when they assured me there was nothing visibly wrong with her. Hana called it a 'sickness of the soul' – a ridiculous sentiment that I quickly checked with the back of my hand.

I should have made a match for her the moment she arrived in Hanover Street. I studied her carefully for a moment: her lips were drawn into a petulant line; her hair, which once glistened, was dimmed; her complexion had grown translucent, like glass. She was losing her bloom. No reputable gentleman would go near her. Why would they? There are fortune hunters aplenty in Liverpool, and they are each comelier than my currency. I would need to buy a husband for her; there was very little choice in the matter.

'You will stay here until I find a husband for you,' I said, attempting to remain calm. 'You will attend balls and public functions again; you will stop hiding in your room like a mouse.'

'If I am unable to return to Speke at this moment, may I visit Charlotte? I have not met my niece yet,' she said calmly.

I poured the tea and sipped it, considering what to do with her. Henrietta *seemed* to wait patiently, but the tapping of her foot under the table betrayed her.

'Very well,' I said finally. 'I can find a suitable husband in your absence. When you return, you will be betrothed.'

Henrietta stirred at this and seemed to rise like an autumn crocus. 'I do not want a husband,' she said boldly.

I felt my jaw tightening. 'I sometimes wonder how you came to be, when your sister is so obliging,' I said, keeping my voice low. 'I can only assume that even a good womb can produce ungrateful whelps.'

'Do not speak of Mama,' she said sharply.

'Do not speak of Mama? Do not speak of my wife? You dare bark orders at me?'

She stood up to leave the breakfast room. 'I will go to Charlotte,' she said, and after a pause, 'and I intend to take Hana with me.'

My stomach lurched, a feeling I was not accustomed to. 'Hana will stay here until your return,' I said, gripping the side of the table.

'But sir,' she said, smiling slightly, 'there will be no women in Hanover Street after my departure. What do *you* want with a lady's maid?'

I suddenly understood her: her contempt, her desire to be gone. She *knew*.

Perhaps she was no longer a child after all.

'Take her then,' I said, contemplating how she could know and what it meant. 'It is of no consequence to me.'

'Thank you,' Henrietta said. 'May I leave the room?' she asked cautiously. 'I want to write to Charlotte directly.'

I brushed her aside with my hand, and she scampered away before I could change my mind.

When I was sure Henrietta had retreated to her bedroom, I took a single cup from the table with the intention of throwing it against the marble fireplace. If all my rage could be contained in a mere cup, I would have already smashed nearly every tea-set in Liverpool. But *this* tea-set belonged to Emma. I stroked the blue flowers, hyacinth, and the gold that rimmed both the cup and the saucer, and I could not bring myself to destroy it. I often shift from grief to regret to resentment, but being aware of this order does not seem to ease it, for I am besieged by treachery and disappointment on all sides. Emma died and left me in charge of two daughters: one as inscrutable as the other. I saved Hana when she was barely ten years old and gave her a comfortable home: she betrayed me by turning one of those daughters against me. It *must* be Hana's betrayal. How else could Henrietta know?

'She's a fucking traitor,' I said aloud. I set the cup carefully on its saucer and rubbed my forehead to calm this relentless sense of outrage that was never far away. Hana was no better than Ned Morgan: no better than a common swindler.

Ned's betrayal cut deeply, but instead of allowing the wound to heal, as I should, I picked at the scab continuously. It served as a reminder, a reminder to be watchful.

Ned was one of my Bluecoat urchins, from the charitable school my grandfather had established near the docks, and which I felt duty bound to continue funding. My ties to the school set me apart from the other Liverpool merchants, for I alone use my wealth to aid in the betterment of the city's poorest inhabitants. Many of the Bluecoat children are orphans, but Ned Morgan was different. He had a mother in Wales who sent him to Liverpool with his father to become a dockworker, but his father, as far as I know, had disappeared in strange circumstances, leaving his son to fend for himself.

Ned was found and taken to the school, where he excelled. He was shrewd with a strong instinct to survive, and this sharpness instantly recommended him to me. Emma had just given birth to Henrietta, and the delivery had very nearly killed her. There would be no more children, no sons. But I consoled myself; there were sons aplenty in Bluecoat School, and I believed Ned deserved to be the first.

I sat back, the front of my head throbbing. Heathcliff would not disappoint me; *he* at least would be loyal.

As though summoned by thought alone, one of the grooms appeared at the door with letters. I beckoned him into the breakfast room and took the correspondence from him. I recognised the handwriting. There were three letters from my overseer and one from Heathcliff. I had not heard from my overseer, Thomas Newton, since the *Othello* had landed in Jamaica five months hence, in which he reported that the ship had safely docked. I was drawn to Heathcliff's letter, since he had resided in my thoughts moments before, but I was eager to learn more about the voyage, and Thomas Newton is always a reliable source. I placed Heathcliff's missive at the bottom of the pile.

'When did these arrive?' I asked the groom.

'Pardon, sir. They all arrived together on the *King James*, which docked yesterday. Will that be all, sir?'

'Yes, go about your duties,' I said, checking the seal before opening the earliest letter, dated October 12th.

New Speke Hall, Clarendon. Jamaica.
Dear Mr Unsworth,

Since informing you of the safe arrival of the Othello, *I have undergone a thorough check of the cargo, as you requested.*

The slaves are in remarkably good health; there is no scurvy present, and they are not overly emaciated. Your man, Heathcliff, reported a single mortality – a female slave. It seems the crew was more severely affected by the voyage than the cargo, as is often the outcome. The captain, Gunning, reports four men lost in storms on the coast of West Africa, a boy who died of his injuries obtained onboard, and the suicide of the ship's surgeon, who had concealed an opium addiction and was driven mad when his supply was diminished. Heathcliff is in possession of his journals, and has intimated that he will destroy them, for it seems the surgeon had questionable ideas about the slave trade. Gunning seems to blame the surgeon for the death of the boy, but this is merely conjecture on my behalf; he has not admitted the man's culpability, although it is evident that the surgeon was not liked by the remaining crew.

The crew is therefore heavily reduced in number, but Gunning insists there are sufficient bodies to manage the Othello *on the return voyage. I am less certain, and I would welcome your instructions on how best to proceed, although I am aware they may not reach me in sufficient time to implement them.*

We will commence the loading of cotton within the month. I anticipate one hundred and fifty tonnes, perhaps more, for, as instructed, I will ensure the new slaves understand their responsibilities to their master.

I hope Henrietta and Charlotte are well, and may I congratulate you on the safe arrival of your first grandchild.

I will write again within the month.

Yours, etc.
Thomas Newton

I was, of course, relieved at the safe arrival of my cargo and the fortune in cotton I was to expect, but six crew dead on the middle passage and the ship still intact? This was unheard of. I would expect to lose one or two on the return voyage to Liverpool, since the men spend nearly a year at sea, but the suicide of the surgeon and the death of the boy gnawed at me. The ship's company do not fucking kill themselves. They stay alive for their cut, for the fortune they will make on their return. Twenty-four men would barely be sufficient to safely navigate my interests. Thomas would need to provide more men.

Something was amiss, and Heathcliff, who I placed on board to facilitate a smooth operation, had evidently fucked up. Had Gunning turned traitor and disposed of those loyal to me? The cut would now be shared among twenty-six instead of thirty-one, although the dead boy's financial gain would have been a small percentage of the overall profit. Had Heathcliff proved himself unfaithful? I struggled with the acknowledgement that I may have misjudged him, for Heathcliff is shackled to me by iron he believes he forged himself.

I held Heathcliff's letter, but one string of questioning at a time; that has always been my approach. Thomas Newton's next letter was written six weeks after the first. Likewise, the seal remained intact.

New Speke Hall, Clarendon. Jamaica.
Dear Mr Unsworth,

*I hope this letter finds you in good health. I have much to acquaint
you with.*

*It seems the slaves were prudently chosen by the deceased surgeon,
although I believe Heathcliff also had a hand in it, for most are hardy
and work from sunrise to sunset under very little duress. Those that
would complain are now too fearful of Heathcliff to protest. This
may have been your motive in sending him to me; perhaps you think I
am too lenient with the slaves? The other men you have sent me during
the last thirty years, Earnshaw, and Johnson, were shrewd merchants
and knew the wealth to be made in treating the slaves firmly but justly
– that they live longer and thus work for longer. Earnshaw fraternised
with the female slaves more than I liked, but he was an honest
gentleman, as was Johnston. I am proud there has never been a slave
rebellion in New Speke; not in the forty years I have been foreman.*

*You are accustomed to my reports, thus I must inform you that
Heathcliff is not cut from the same stone as the others, despite his
links to Earnshaw. He breeds ill-feeling in others, and he is very per-
suasive. However, the wives of the other plantation foremen, such as
Gabe Pearson's wife, appear seduced by his foreignness. He is aloof
and cold towards them, but the women care not. He turns down
invitations and responds facetiously to their questions, and they seem
to like him more for his indifference! The Negro women are more
astute, for they despise him.*

I am not certain what exactly took place on the Othello, *and Gunning
will confess nothing, but in the week after the ship's arrival, the slave
women would hiss and spit at Heathcliff, and then take flight before
he could beat them. Heathcliff is very determined, as I am certain
you are aware, for he found those responsible and ordered their teeth
knocked out to stop their 'damned hissing'. The women anticipated a*

whipping, and thus did not expect to have their jaws wrenched open and be threatened with a claw-hammer. I intervened, since slaves need sustenance to work, therefore removing all their teeth would be a foolish and profitless punishment. I also believed the punishment to be severe, and perhaps entirely unwarranted.

From the brief time I have known Heathcliff, I can see he has many advantageous qualities: his resolve, his intelligence, and his capacity for endurance. The voyage has weakened many of the crew, with some taking to their bed for days, including Gunning, but Heathcliff is robust in mind and in body. I can thus perceive your reasons for favouring him, but I must be candid regardless of your high opinion of him, for we have a shared history that I hope will allow me to be impertinent. When I prevented Heathcliff's order from being implemented, his reaction convinced me of two things: his cruelty, and his vindictiveness. He cannot tolerate subjugation; he will be his own master and will accept no other. I do not mean to question your reasoning. I only mean to advise care and watchfulness. Do not turn your back on him, Samuel.

To appease him, and to prevent being killed in my own bed, I hung the ringleader before all the other women. They wept and howled but did not provoke Heathcliff. He watched dispassionately from the veranda. Hanging slaves is not a practice I relish; I can think of only a few others who have met the same fate at my hands.

The following morning, the dead slave still swung from the cotton tree in the yard. I ordered two of my men to cut her down and bury her, since her presence lowered the spirits of the other slaves and leaving her without a Christian burial was abhorrent to me. Simpson, the more forward of the two, informed me that Heathcliff had forbidden them from cutting down the body. This angered me, and I repeated my order more firmly, which they both obeyed.

Despite Heathcliff's resilience and quickness, for he has learnt in four months what most would spend years perfecting – such as the governing of the slaves, the processing of the cotton, and the day-to-day running of a large plantation – I must admit that I look forward to his departure. I believe he would be a capable foreman in many aspects, but if given such a role he would crush those beneath him and attempt to destroy those above him.

I beseech you not to think me impudent or receive my advice in a differing spirit to the one in which it is offered.

Yours, etc.
Thomas Newton

Thomas has always been a stickler; he would find troubled waters in a drought, but I have always listened to his advice. I have not always followed it, but I have always listened.

I thought perhaps Heathcliff had turned savage; nothing like Earnshaw, whose appetites were of a more lascivious nature. I knew Heathcliff could be wolfish when necessary, but his impulses were in check at Hanover Street, and thus he was not provided with the necessary environment for brutality to flourish. He took a dislike to Hana. She threatened him with her curses the day before he set sail, and he calmly smashed her nose with his fist. It pleased me, for she is a churlish whore who should be regularly reminded of her place. Heathcliff's new savagery suited me in ways I could not explain to Thomas. The foreman of a new plantation must be man enough to do whatever it takes to subdue the blacks, since processing sugar cane, which is my new venture, is a jaunt compared to picking cotton.

I opened Thomas' third and final letter, dated January 2nd, having already decided to discount the sermon within it.

New Speke Hall, Clarendon. Jamaica.
Dear Mr Unsworth,

Your necessities are embarked, sir. The Othello *will set sail on the morning tide. You can expect the arrival of the ship to fall before the month of July. God willing.*

I have proceeded as usual. I thought it prudent to bolster the crew with three of my own men, which is all that I can spare. There are now twenty-seven souls on board, which should be sufficient for the voyage over the Atlantic. I would be obliged if you could find an occupation for them during their stay in Liverpool and send them back on the next available ship.

The waters near Jamaica have been free of pirates of late, therefore only a tempest could interfere with the safe arrival of the cargo. Heathcliff has also written to you, and although I am not certain what his letter contains, I must assume that he will send you a report on Captain Gunning. In my mind, sir, Gunning will not prove treacherous. He has often spoken of what befell Captain Cox and your man, Morgan. I do not think he wishes for the same fate. I still affirm that Heathcliff's interests are selfish, thus I would not take his word as God's truth, if I may be plain with you.

Heathcliff is eager to be gone, which makes me question his commitment to the life you intend for him. I do not think the West Indies will be his home. He has grown wistful and speaks of an old love and the enemies he longs to return to. His savagery faces east, for he raves about the revenge he will inflict on his adversaries, now he is able. His focus on the slaves has taken a welcome turn, for he no longer baits them or stirs them to a violence that I am then obliged to punish them for. I have done my very best with him, Samuel, but he has proved to be the most challenging charge thus far.

I would be grateful if you could inform me of the Othello*'s safe arrival in Liverpool. I have enclosed details of the weight and quality of the cotton on board; less any should go astray between here and there. As I have already intimated, I believe Gunning is* *honourable, however it is always prudent to be cautious in these matters.*

Yours, etc.
Thomas Newton

'Sir?'

I looked up from Thomas' correspondence.

'Sir?'

'Yes, yes, what is it?' I said, placing his letter and The *Othello*'s inventory on the table. 'Oh, it's you again. Am I no longer Papa? What tales has Hana been telling?' Despite my direct question, I decided that in truth I did not want Henrietta to answer it. 'It is of no importance, not now,' I added quickly. 'Is that the letter to Charlotte?' I asked, pointing to the envelope in her hand.

'Yes, I will send it immediately. I came to inform you that Hana did not protest about departing Hanover Street. In fact, she is so looking forward to it, that she wishes to sleep in my room from now on. We have grown very close, you see, sir.'

After a pause, during which I made no attempt to compose myself, I stood and beckoned her to me. She had never been hit, and therefore she did not think to turn and run, for she had no concept of pain from a father's hand.

I did not strike her hard, but the force was enough to make her cower in shock.

'You are mine, just as Hana is mine. You are both my property, and if you ever defy or challenge me again, you will know what it is to pine for a husband, girl. Who are you to assay me? Do you assume that our familial bond will save you? Nothing will preserve you if you continue to bait me, do you hear?'

Henrietta was pressed against the far wall, with a table and four chairs between us. I returned to my seat and continued as though our quarrel had not taken place, an action intended to puzzle and bewilder.

I picked up Heathcliff's letter and waved it at her, my tone suddenly jovial. 'You may be interested in this. You and Heathcliff were as thick as thieves before he departed.'

Henrietta's eyes grew wild. 'I do not know what you mean, sir.'

'*Sir*, Henrietta? I am your loving father.'

'Papa,' she said quickly.

'You do not know what I mean? Of course, you do. Did I imagine you teaching him how to speak like a gentleman? Or was it Titania, or perhaps Ariel, who was responsible for his transformation?'

When she did not answer, I felt my accustomed frustration, but I did not move from my seat.

'Well?' I said, pushing her to answer.

'Yes, I taught him.'

'Is that all you can say? *Yes, I taught him*,' I said, mimicking her now feeble voice.

She began to cry, and I swore at the heavens for providing me with such a fucking whelp. I was about to banish her from my sight and put an end to it when she unexpectedly moved across the room and kneeled at my feet.

'Papa, please do not open his letter,' she pleaded.

'Why?' I asked, suddenly interested. 'What will I find in it?'

She shook her head and ran from the room in a squall of skirts and my fortune in ribbons.

I was incredulous. Had she taken a fancy to him like those idiotic plantation wives? She is as stupid as she is unseasoned; Heathcliff would rather tear out his own eyes than even feign an interest in her. It was no wonder he so readily took his leave. But the thought of Henrietta bestowing her affections so readily, and on a misbegotten whoreson, troubled me despite my fondness for Heathcliff.

When he sought me out after Ned's treachery, I of course identified him as the street urchin abandoned and then saved by my old associate. Earnshaw was a better man than I, for I would have cast him off and allowed him to die in the street.

In truth, I did not expect the boy to still be breathing, and when I instructed Earnshaw where he might find him, I was amazed that he boy was brought back alive, although flea ridden and matted. I questioned Earnshaw's motives and told him he was a fool to think he could merely install the boy at Wuthering Heights and pretend he had nothing to do with him, but I have benefitted from his sentimentality, for Heathcliff has been useful.

I stared at Heathcliff's letter a while before opening it.

If he had turned traitor, I would reacquaint him with his lodgings in the Tower. Sentiment should never overrule sense. I owed Earnshaw when he was living – he was a loyal overseer for a time – but I owed him nothing now he was dead. I owed his bastard even less.

I used a butter knife to hack at the envelope, for there was no seal.

Clarendon, Jamaica.
Dear Sir,

I trust you received my last correspondence, which I sent before we undertook the middle passage, thus I only need acquaint you with the happenings of recent months. I will do so sparingly.

Before I commence, I am aware that Newton has written to you on more than one occasion, and I will not waste time and tide dwelling on details that I am certain he has taken great pains to re-fashion. I trust your judgment, and your sufficient understanding of both our characters, to separate the shit from the soil, so to speak.

I know you will want to hear of Gunning; let me put you at ease. He is no traitor. He is many other things: phlegmatic and puffed up, with a tendency to enjoy the sound of his own supposals, which we had to endure at length since we are all captives together at sea, but you know me; I laughed at him often and he despises me for it. This hatred is mutual, of course. He is far too cock-sure, and were it not for his experience at sea, I would happily have dashed his brains out. But he navigated us through rough waters along the coast of Sierra Leone. He can exert himself effectively when he deems it necessary. He is in essence naturally indolent with only brief sparks of fire; thus, I cannot certify any plot against you. None fore-laid by the captain, at least. Your cargo is safe.

Your reputation, you will be grieved to discover, is less secure as long as the surgeon's journals are in existence. Avery was an imposter and had no place on a slave ship. He planned to undo the trade one link at a time and wrote lies about the management of the slaves. Much has been carved from very little, thus I will drown his blasted books on the return voyage. I hope this action serves as proof of my loyalty to you, for if these journals were put in the wrong hands, they would contribute to the loss of your world in its entirety. I sense the imminent end of this trade, but this end should be delayed, for there is much to lose, for both of us.

If all is well, we are set to depart on the morning tide, and I look forward to seeing Liverpool and perhaps Yorkshire once more. Jamaica, its unendurable heat, and its accursed inhabitants, I will gladly leave behind.

There is one further point I must raise with you. It is a sensitive business regarding Miss Unsworth. I am grateful for her efforts in polishing my speech and manners, but it would be to her benefit if she were elsewhere when I arrive in Hanover Street. I am afraid she took to me in a way I could never reciprocate, due to my position and status, and my own inclination against her. My soul, such as it is, hankers for another. I am sure you understand me.

I look forward to meeting you again, now that my education is completed.

Yours, etc.
Heathcliff

I stood and moved to the window, still holding Heathcliff's letter. The afternoon was dank and colourless. A fleet of umbrellas sailed by, all black, and no one ambled or stopped or lifted their eyes from the pavement.

Liverpool was gunpowder grey, which made me briefly think of how green the grass at Speke always looks after rainfall. Then I thought of how green Henrietta is. If there were new ribbons to purchase and balls aplenty, she would steep my name in shit and not give it a moment's consideration.

I had assumed she viewed Heathcliff merely as an oddity, as a source of entertainment, as a necessary evil to keep her from my enemies, although I am certain she never realised the threat. To offer herself so freely to a person of such little consequence in the world … I could not fathom it.

But she is an Unsworth, despite her defects, and if she is on heat, then I must direct her towards a more suitable mate.

Heathcliff could never be a suitable husband to Henrietta, but he had proved necessary, and thus in pecuniary terms, he would be a good match for somebody. I planned to reward him, despite his ill-advised threat about the journals. Did he really believe that one report would halt a trade that is so fixed in the minds and pockets of the nation? The journals meant nothing; they were written by a discredited suicide with an opium addiction. Perhaps Heathcliff's education was not quite as complete as he believed.

However, his account of Gunning was comparable with Thomas', which eased my fears. It seems that one act of treachery breeds an entire host of potential Judases, but I had to be certain of Gunning, and it is impossible to say whether Heathcliff's presence on the *Othello* may have put an end to any designs against me. There was no wonder he despised Heathcliff so!

Yes, all was in order on the *Othello*; Earnshaw's bastard had been a prosperous undertaking. I had played my hand well.

I folded the letters and went directly to my study, where I

locked them securely in my desk. I had no engagements until the afternoon, and Heathcliff's letter and the quarrel with Henrietta had roused me. With my prick pressed against my breeches, I summoned the butler and told him to bring Hana to me.

To fill the time between then and her arrival, I commenced writing a notice to be placed in Williamson's Liverpool Advertiser the following morning, requesting the services of an experienced and respectable lady's maid. I stated that I would expect absolute loyalty and discretion.

I assumed that having acquired Hana as a child, she would always be bound to me, that she, above all others, would not betray me. I saved her, and was this all the return I was to receive? She would have died next to her dam in the dark, devoured by rats, if I had not plucked her. And she repaid me by turning my daughter against me.

All desire had now left me, and when the knock came, followed by the customary 'Yes, Massa?' in that enticing, baiting accent of hers, I felt nothing.

The *Othello* docked on August 29th , a month later than Thomas had forecast. I had feared another plot and positioned men in Crosby and Formby as a precaution, but there was no need; the ship sailed into the Old Dock early that morning, and everything seemed to be in order. There was no treason to manage, and no planned shipwreck this time; merely the legitimate unloading and settling of accounts. My relief was immediate – I swaggered between the Old Dock and the Customs House, ready to send the world spinning on its axis. I was elated and prepared to reward and praise everyone involved in the venture. When I returned to Hanover Street with my associates, I uncorked a 1762 Burgundy, and we drank it from my finest crystal. I sent for another bottle for Gunning and Heathcliff, who I expected to see later that day.

Henrietta was still encamped with Charlotte; thus, I did not have to deal with her mawkish regard for Heathcliff or his mortification. The months since her going had been serene in comparison with the clamour that had preceded her departure. Her screams when she realised what had happened to Hana, that she would not be joining her, still sound in my head when I am alone, but otherwise, I do not think of her. Charlotte wrote to me, not long after I'd sent Henrietta on her way, suggesting that it might be 'best for everyone' if she remained with her for the entire summer season, that she would take it upon herself to 'introduce her to society', to find a 'suitable match' for her, and so on. It suited me to have Hanover Street to myself again, devoid of female frills and frippery. Hana sometimes occupies my thoughts, but there are whores aplenty in Liverpool, and they always send me the best. I considered purchasing a further two that evening, for Gunning and Heathcliff, as a reward for all those months at sea, but when Heathcliff appeared, he was alone, and he was not the unfledged apprentice I had sent forth into the world. He was taller, broader, and carried himself with the authority of a much older and more experienced man. I was reminded of Earnshaw as a youth, for the likeness was now obvious.

'Heathcliff, I almost did not know you,' I said, staring at him. He did not baulk under my scrutiny, which galled me. I offered my hand, and when he took it, his hand swallowed mine like an ocean engulfing a ship. It was a relief that Henrietta was not there to see Heathcliff's transformation. She had humiliated herself, and me, enough.

'Thank you,' he said, sitting, despite not receiving an invitation to do so. 'I am excessively glad to be back.'

I remained standing, taking in his weight and breadth. I could not overpower this new Heathcliff.

'Will you not sit down, sir?' he asked, gesturing to my *own* fucking chair.

'Forgive me,' I said, standing taller. 'You are much changed.'

'Yes, I am not what I was,' he said. His accent was different; there was a foreignness about it that I could not place. 'You sent me across the ocean, after all,' he continued. 'I hope I was of service to you in that brave new world, for I am, of course, indebted to you for allowing me to see it.'

I welcomed this show of gratitude, for I realised its initial absence had set me on edge. I positioned myself in the chair opposite him, with my desk between us.

'You have been most useful,' I said, feeling calmer. 'You secured my interests and deterred those that might have deceived me. I hope your service will continue now that you are on land once more.'

His response was quick. 'I must first be paid for services rendered. Is that not customary before committing to further employment?'

I had not anticipated such a direct demand, but now it was made, I had to address it. He was bold for a bastard son of a slave-whore.

'Of course,' I said. 'You will be handsomely rewarded for your efforts. You safely delivered a treasure chest in cotton, but that amount of cargo will take time to value.'

'How much time?' he asked instantly. 'I mean to be away within the week.'

I recalled Thomas' letter: *I do not think the West Indies will be his home.* I began to feel the creeping heat in my chest that always precedes a loss of control which, since the Henrietta and Hana affair, I have endeavoured to check.

'Away within a week? Away where?' I asked, remarkably calmly I thought. 'I sent you to New Speke so that you could, within the year, manage my new plantation in Barbados. There will be a fortune to be made there, Heathcliff.'

'But what would I do with that fortune, trapped on an island, an infernal scalding-house, on the other side of the world?' he asked. 'For *this* is my world, and I mean to reclaim it.'

I regarded him a moment, whilst attempting to control the anger rising within me.

'What is the meaning of this?' I asked, finally.

'I simply do not wish to return to the West Indies,' he said, shrugging, which further infuriated me. 'I have a different design.'

'Pray, what design is that Heathcliff? Or should I address you as *Mr* Heathcliff hitherto?' I asked, gripping the edge of the desk. 'What the fuck is this? I will not be dictated to by a bastard.'

He smiled at me then, deliberately disregarding my ill-humour. 'I have destroyed the surgeon's journals, as promised,' he said, studying his hands casually. 'They will not resurface.'

'The journals were of no consequence; you held them above their importance,' I said, breathing hard. 'They were written by a man who ruined himself, who was held in contempt by the crew.'

'Is that what Newton said?' he asked, with a grin I wanted to slice from his face with a blade.

'Ah, now you are a fucking sphinx, are you?' I said. 'What new Heathcliff is this?'

'There is no riddle. I am merely suggesting that Newton did not know Avery; he heard only Gunning's account of events. But it is of no importment,' he said, waving the subject away with his hand. 'For the journals are at the bottom of the Atlantic.'

He reached into his pocket and placed a bundle of letters on his knee.

'What are those?' I asked, alert to a potential threat.

He opened one of the letters and held it up. 'Do you recognize the hand?'

I struck my fists on a side table and then flung it against the near wall. I knew precisely whose hand it was.

'The stupid, ungrateful slut!' I said, rising. 'I sent her to Charlotte, and she is fortunate. If she were here, I would hang her in the street for all to see what a fucking brat I spawned, a disgrace to the Unsworth name.'

I paced the room, circling Heathcliff. I was in some paroxysm of fury; I could not contain it. I wanted to order Heathcliff's death right there and then, despite my old regard for him. My men were not far, only in the sitting room, but he must have sensed this danger, for he proceeded to make it impossible for me to destroy him.

'I have other letters that are not on my person, with instructions for them to be sent immediately to the Liverpool Advertiser should something happen to me,' he said, utterly composed. 'They are all in the same vein: sickly, uninvited declarations of love. She thought me a hero of romance: a fabulous notion of my character! I could not perceive a rational thought in that empty head of hers, and she persisted in this absurd state for many months. I have ten letters in all,' he said, placing the bundle back in his pocket. 'I believe Hana attempted to sway her, but Henrietta was too steeped in her delusion to be easily freed. I, of course, made no reply to these assaults. I made no response to her slavish attempts to court me. You are fortunate that I am an honourable man.'

I had been entirely played and undone by a boy I had treated as a son, and a daughter I, at that moment, wished had never been born. The knowledge that Hana knew Heathcliff for what he was, also pressed heavily on me. All anger had left me, and I suddenly felt every day of my fifty-five years.

'Where will you go?' I asked, collapsing onto my chair.

'I will return to Wuthering Heights, settle my score with Hindley, and marry Catherine Earnshaw. You will never see me again, I assure you.'

'Catherine Earnshaw?' I asked, leaning forward.

'Yes, what of it?' he asked curtly. It was the first time his composure seemed to slip. I briefly had the upper hand.

'Earnshaw's daughter?' I asked, trying to provoke him. 'You once asked me if I knew your parentage, do you remember?'

'I do.'

'Do you still hanker for your origins?'

'I do not.' He answered, firmly. 'For I am my own man. I will fashion my own history.'

He glared at me, and I caught a glimpse of the 'old' Heathcliff; the Heathcliff who could crack my skull open. Yes, he knew the truth of it, I realised, and he did not care. I hoped I could heap agonies on him, that I could reveal a truth that would devastate him and send him scurrying, but of course he knew. He need only gaze in a mirror to see it.

I opened a drawer that contained a host of bank bills.

'How much will it take to be rid of you?' I asked.

'I will destroy the letters immediately, all bar one in case you decide to come after me, for the sum of £10,000,' he said evenly. 'I will accept no less than that. Do not forget that I know you have eight times that amount.'

'Hana, in all her damned slave wisdom, knew what you were, and I beat her for it,' I said, rubbing my temples, for my head suddenly throbbed. I wanted him gone.

'Yes, you did,' he said. 'Where is she? Did you murder her or dismiss her?'

I would not make Heathcliff my confederate, I would not admit that I placed Hana on a ship to Sierra Leone where, I have heard, they treat their own slaves worse than we do theirs.

I picked up my quill and scratched my signature, stiffening the hair on my arms and quickening my pulse. My head throbbed in keeping with it.

'Take it,' I spat, throwing the bill at him. 'You have made an enemy of me, Heathcliff. If I ever see you again, be assured that I will kill you.'

Heathcliff

Liverpool and Gimmerton
September 1783

I left Hanover Street directly, cutting through the park lest he was watching from a window. I knew Unsworth's ilk – his web extended far, even to the cut-throats of Gibraltar Street, and I had revealed too much of my plans. It was madness to speak so freely, but how could I not when I had barely uttered her name in three years? I pressed my hands into the trunk of a tree, a sycamore, and pushed so the pain would scatter my indignation like sparks from a fire.

Unsworth had smiled like a fool when I appeared at his door. I was the wanderer-apprentice, the nameless heir he craved. The son-in-law he would rather die by inches than admit, but Henrietta was a poor surrogate for Cathy; a nettling, infantile bitch whose eyes I would have happily turned as dark as mine. I leaned against the trunk, cursing how readily I had unfolded my narrative before him like a damned book-merchant.

I shut my eyes tight and tried to set aside my error with Unsworth. I needed to root myself to the present, to the sycamore I leaned against, to the earth below, to the blood pooling in my palms. When I opened my eyes, I would be in control of myself again.

Who knows how long I stood there. Voices drifted on the breeze and were then silent. A horse and carriage hurried past; a bell chimed. When I finally opened my eyes, the morning clouds had begun to disperse, and I was careful not to reveal myself under the dappled light of the branches as I slowly removed bits of bark from my palms.

I stayed hidden and watched the house, just as Henrietta used to watch the park from her window. In another life I could be watching her, watching me, and the thought first excited me and then chilled me. It recalled the last time I saw Anne Feather, exposed and wretched at a window that shook with her distress. There was the dream I shared with Avery on the *Othello*, of the hand breaking through glass and its horrible, desperate grasping. Then I was, once again, inside the window-less cell in the Tower...

I pressed my head against the bark and felt its undulations on my face. I closed my eyes for a moment, allowing the mixture of shadow and light to fill my vision, and when I opened them, I was returned to the present. I thought only weak minds could be so easily uprooted, a mind such as Avery's. But I found myself drifting more and more in recent weeks. I narrowed my eyes and focused on the house, with its too-handsome façade and light-filled windows, and waited.

No-one emerged for twenty minutes.

When the door did suddenly open, it was not an assassin after all; it was merely the kitchen boy. He held a letter and looked disappointed when he turned it in his hand to check the seal. He scanned the road quickly, jumped the steps and ran in the direction of Paradise Street.

Was this a death sentence or a warrant for my arrest? Either way, I could not return to Madoc House.

I deposited the bill in the bank on Castle Street – the furthest establishment of that sort from my lodgings. The clerk paused when he saw the amount, but his hesitation was momentary, for I had identification papers and I was no longer the ragged vagabond of old. I had Ned Morgan and the Unsworth whore to thank for that.

'Please sit, Mr Heathcliff,' he said, studying Unsworth's signature carefully. 'I will be a few moments. I must check the vault, for we may not have that sum available. I assume you would like the amount in ready money, since you do not have an account with us.'

'Yes, that is exactly right,' I said.

He disappeared behind a panel, and I leaned back so that I could watch the door and view the room. Clerks sat at their desks, rearranging papers, or perusing documents. The manager snaked between them, his head high and his eyes lowered. One of the clerks was idle, but he rose from his chair when he saw his overseer and shuffled to the door, ready to greet the next man to walk through it. What a soulless existence! I would never be bound to another man again; no man would ever bark orders at me or abuse me or grind me down. I would return as Hindley's superior, and as for Linton, I was now his equal in wealth and rank. I knew Cathy would be vexed by my disappearance, that she had not allowed her scant fancy for that insipid faintling to usurp her feelings for me.

'Mr Heathcliff?'

The clerk had returned.

'Excuse me,' I said, standing. 'I was far away for a moment.'

I signed the required papers and placed my new fortune into the satchel provided. I did not hold the notes in my hand for long lest I betrayed myself and revealed the truth of my situation — that my future, my very existence, was in those papers.

The clerk stared at me.

'Was there something else?' I asked.

'You must be wary of thieves, Mr Heathcliff,' he said.

'Do not concern yourself,' I said sharply, offering no further explanation.

The clerk bid me good day, but I was already at the door and did not return the sentiment.

I left Liverpool just before nightfall, on a horse I extorted from one of Ned Morgan's old associates. He would have parted with his own life to be rid of me, I was certain of it, but I settled for his most prized stallion and the pistol from his own pocket. I would lodge a ball in any man or woman sent to hinder me.

I rode away from the setting sun with a satchel full of sterling and the pistol pressed against my thigh like a promise, and I had never felt so alive, so vital. All my suffering had led to this moment. I flew past inns warm with candlelight and houses with their inhabitants enveloped in the comfort of sleep, and I did not envy their peace. I was impelled by an urgency that first took hold on the *Othello* and which nearly drove me overboard, but the distance between us lessened with every beat of the horse's hooves, and there was quicksilver in my veins. She must have known I was close: how could she not, when all my thoughts were fixed on her?

Derbyshire unrolled like plated silver in the moonlight. It was a tapestry of my past, for I walked this tract with Earnshaw nearly a lifetime hence and I used the same road on that accursed night three years ago, plagued by a storm of vengeance fore and aft. The wind that night was diabolical – the way it compelled me and drove me into the hands of Ned Morgan. There was no such bluster now. The air was mild and there was only the screeching of owls and the pounding of hooves on dry earth.

Though the horse was slick with sweat, we carried on through the night, until day broke over the moor, smothering the shadows from every thicket and river, every hill and valley, until this golden landscape was spun into the story of Cathy and me. Every rock, every coil of river, the ground beneath and the air above, all glistened their welcome. I recalled my very first time in this valley, the sounds of skylark and grouse, Earnshaw a constant presence, guiding me, protecting me. My heart leapt.

I was home.

The moment I rode into Gimmerton the weather turned.

It began as drizzle, but then a grey sheet descended and Main Street's yorkstone dwellings darkened like wet lead. But it was English rain, *Yorkshire* rain, and how I had longed for it! Jamaica, with its unbearable heat, was a place of stagnation and madness, with no repose from the air that seemed to hang upon me like chains. Here water imbued the atmosphere, and the droplets of rain on my coat, my hands, my eyelashes, were as light as thistledown.

The Yorkshire natives were unperturbed by the summer rain; it was as akin to them as their own skin. They continued with their day and paid no heed to the weather, but *my* presence they could not ignore. They were the same devils that appraised me when I was first presented to them, as a lad of no more than seven years. They had not seen my like before or since – or so their expressions implied. They measured and weighed and conferred, whilst I remained upright and coldly wished the fiends a good morning.

I recognised one person – the butcher, although I could not recall his name. He stood at the gates of his shambles not far from the Black Bull Inn.

'Aye, lad, I remember you,' he said, expanding his chest like a robin under threat. 'I said you would be back one day, and here you are.'

'Yes, here I am,' I said. I took him by surprise and dismounted the horse in one easy movement. He stepped back as I approached. When I was a bairn he was as tall and as broad as the trunk of an oak, but now, as I hanged over him, his bole was bent.

'A soothsayer *and* a butcher,' I said, baring my teeth in a humourless smile. 'Tell me soothsayer, who am I?'

'You are not the same,' he said, faltering. 'I will not speak with you.'

'Who am I?' I asked again, leaning in so close that the burst blood vessels on his nose and cheeks were like inlets.

'No,' he said, lowering his head and stepping away. 'I was mistaken.'

'Yes, you were,' I said, wiping the rain from his shoulder with my hand. He endured it and did not flinch, although his eyes were lowered, and his jaw was rigid. 'But if your mistake should reach Hindley, then I will be back this evening, and perhaps we can become better acquainted?'

I expected him to skulk back to his blood and offal, but he saw something or some person up the street, and his smile, when it came, was self-satisfied and gloating.

'I warrant *he* knows you,' he said, pointing.

I stared at the butcher for a moment, unable to wrench my eyes away, for I could guess who was standing on the brow of the hill, and I did not wish to see him.

I turned and ascended the horse, cursing the butcher and anyone else who dared raise their head. I was aware of the Black Bull Inn and the figure standing before it, but the inn and its inhabitants were no longer my axle, thus I averted my eyes and fixed my sights on the moors rising in the distance.

I could see Feather emerging into the road from the margin of my vision, but I spurred the horse onwards, with the intention of galloping past him. The fool stood in my way, like a dog confronted with the end of a pistol. My horse reared up, and it required all my skill to remain on its back.

'Feather – what in the devil are you doing? Do you wish to be trampled?'

The butcher was still outside his premises and a sodden crowd had begun to gather.

Feather was thinner than I remembered – or perhaps eroded. His skin was as worn as limestone after a hundred years of rainfall. I could not account for his transformation, nor did I care. Yorkshire rain could drown your senses, but mine were as sharp as my intent, and the moors, partially obscured by a veil of cloud and water, were more real than this carrion that stood in my way.

'Out of my way,' I said. 'I have no business with you.'

'I shall not, Heathcliff,' he said. The use of my name startled me in a way I did not expect, and the innkeeper saw it. 'Aye, I know your name, lad,' he continued. 'You may look the gentleman now, but I know what churns within you. I *know* you.'

I thought of Anne, and began to suspect why this man, who was once kind to me, should demand my attention.

'You know nothing of me,' I said, pulling my attention from the moors and onto Feather. 'I have grappled with horrors since our last meeting, and I do not need *your* troubles heaped upon me.'

'My troubles?' he said, his mouth agape like a cadaver's. 'Nay, do not speak of my troubles.'

The crowd thickened and grew until it was nearly upon me. I recalled the bonfires and the urchins and immediately recoiled.

'Is she dead?' I asked, staring at Feather, for the milksop was weeping.

'You murdered her,' he said, 'and I want vengeance.'

I wanted to say that I grieved for Anne, that for a time she was a mother to me, that I warned him not to stop the laudanum too suddenly, but his accusation hardened me.

'That is a dangerous charge, Feather,' I said, speaking loud enough so that the crowd could hear my every word. 'I could have you in front of the magistrate for making such a claim against a gentleman.'

He looked at me closely and saw his disadvantage for the first time. The crowd backed away slightly, and any doubt I may have felt was gone. I was the lad he remembered, but he could no longer hope to subdue me, any more than he could quell lightning.

'You say I murdered her – where is your evidence?' I said, boring into him. 'Did I strangle her in the marketplace? Did I cut her throat in the church? Did I throw her down the stairs of the inn?' I paused, and then struck a blow I knew would dissolve the last of him. 'Did I creep into her chamber when she was indisposed, and break her body with a poker?'

His jaw slackened. He looked for aid amongst the crowd, but none was offered.

I leaned over him and spoke quietly. 'Your wife despised you; do you know that? She *despised* you.'

His face twisted into a grimace of what I knew must be excruciating pain, for I had given voice to his darkest fear.

'I did not lay a hand on your wife,' I said loudly. 'If you make that claim again, I will work within the confines of the law to end you. I will not be meddled with, do you hear?'

Feather continued to stand and gawp, waking within me a furious temper. I rode up alongside him and and knocked him down with a kick I knew would put an end to his paltry notions of revenge.

I did not look back as I galloped away, although I could imagine the outrage, the shock that I left behind, and for the first time since leaving Liverpool, I was fearful. I had not expected to see Robert Feather, and his accusation still pressed on my chest. Anne was dead. What other trouble would I encounter at the Heights? It had been three years. I had traversed the oceans in that time. Could I expect life in the Heights to be fixed, spell-stopped like Prospero's enemies?

There was a line of light on the horizon, beneath a rack of dark cloud, and I aimed for it. I rode towards the light, the shelf of sky heavy on my shoulders. I had nearly forgotten the Yorkshire sky; the expanse of it, how you could see the storm clouds rolling across it like a vast wave. Yes, I could see what was coming. I wanted to howl to the elements, to ride the horse until its heart ceased, for I knew, I cannot explain how, but I knew – Cathy was gone.

Wuthering Heights, in her absence, was merely a house – a thing of stone and mortar.

I searched for signs of Nelly, that she might gather up three years and weave them into one of her narratives, but there was no woman's touch there: the garden was a wilderness, and the apples were scattered amongst the grass like erring stars. The stone-step was black with the tread of boots; Nelly would scrub that step anew each day, even on Sundays when no visitors were permitted.

It was a drab homecoming.

Hindley's vociferating could be heard from the gate: slurred curses and cries, followed by the sound of a chair or a table splinting against the tiled floor. It focused my mind, and for a moment, I did not dwell on Cathy and Nelly's desertion and what it could mean. Hindley, at least, seemed unchanged. I could hardly believe the ease of it all, the degradation I only needed to water, not sow. But even the damned could be aided along the path to perdition, and his lack of resistance would make acquiring Wuthering Heights as simple as taking a nest of lapwings.

Joseph opened the door, and when I saw that sermonizing reprobate, all my enmity returned.

'Ah, Joseph,' I said. 'Has God not called you home yet?'

Before he could reply or register his shock, I pushed past him and entered the hall, following the voices I heard from outside. Entering Wuthering Heights again was like skimming backwards through a book, but the main characters were blotted out. This erasing of the past unnerved me, but I'd be damned if I showed it.

Joseph trailed behind me, apparently speechless, for the first time in his cursed existence.

'Is Mr Earnshaw home, Joseph?' I asked, knowing exactly which room his was in.

'Aye, but yah can nay make him worse than he ready is, so return yah t'hell, wert yah belong.'

My laugh hushed the voices in the antechamber.

'Oh, I am already in hell, Joseph, until I see Cathy again.'

The fiend grinned like a harbinger of some doom, but I held his throat and hissed in his ear. 'I know she is not here; I do not need *you* to tell me that.'

If she had truly forsaken me, I would smear the flagstones with Hindley's blood and point the pistol to my own head, for what would be the purpose of existence if she had deserted me?

I released Joseph and calmed the tumult within me. I would enter the room with force, or I would not enter at all.

There were four men inside, including Hindley. The ante-chamber was now a gaming room – a card table was laid out in the centre. The edges of the chamber were a graveyard of table legs, broken chairs, and smashed glass.

'Gentlemen,' I said, surveying the disorder. 'Am I correct in assuming that Mr Earnshaw is a sore loser at cards?'

Hindley was slumped on the table with his back to me, but he attempted to twist his neck in my direction. If he recognised me, he made no sign of it; his head rested on the table once more, and the blindness of drink descended, rendering him senseless.

'I see he is losing badly,' I said, removing my coat. 'But, and this is what troubles me gentlemen, how is he to preserve his measly fortune if he is insensible?'

The men glanced at one another, and I used this pause to stride towards the table. I seized Hindley by the collar and lifted him from his chair, carrying him one-handed to the corner of the room that most resembled a domestic charnel house. I dropped him there, amongst the wooden arms and legs, and returned to the table.

'Gentlemen, it is time for conversation,' I said, taking Hindley's place. 'I will speak plainly. How much have you extorted from Mr Earnshaw? Come, be direct with me.'

The largest of the three men stood, tipping his chair over.

'You are that Heathcliff, the brat old Earnshaw brought from Liverpool. I remember you. Do not meddle in Hindley's business, for it has nowt to do with you.'

'I have been in the company of worse men than you,' I said, rising from my seat. 'Hindley's business has a great deal to do with me – it will be mine even before he is writhing in hell. I detest that man with every thread of my being,' I said, glaring at Hindley's twisted frame. 'My interest in his debts is purely selfish, I assure you. Now, I shall ask again, how much have you extorted from Mr Earnshaw?'

He recovered his chair clumsily and sat himself amongst his associates. I returned to my seat but remained alert.

'Well? Do you need to discuss a suitably fabulous amount?' I asked, not concealing my contempt.

The degenerates whispered amongst themselves whilst I watched them invent a fortune.

'Hindley owes us five hundred pound,' the largest man declared. 'Five hundred a piece.'

'Try again,' I said, my eyes fixed on him.

'That is the total of his debt,' he persisted, but with less audacity.

'Try again,' I repeated.

'Four hundred pound a piece; we won't take no less.'

'Allow me to make a suggestion,' I began, removing three hundred pounds in notes from my inner pocket. 'You will receive these notes, which you may grapple over at your own leisure. You will wring no more from me. If your greed compels you to complain, then I will not cut your throats, but I will refer your claim to the magistrate, who will require proof of your debt. Do you have proof?'

The men glanced at one another.

'Do you have proof?'

The spokesman wished me dead, that much I could certify, but I would not acquiesce. Not yet.

'Are you all tenants of Mr Earnshaw?'

This unsettled them: they were like rabbits suddenly aware of the goshawk above them.

'When I am the proprietor here, you shall all be my tenants. I imagine Mr Earnshaw has not been diligent in collecting rents, but I will, of course, put the accounts in order as a matter of urgency.'

'Damn you!' the brute shouted, leaning forward.

'You are too late, I am afraid.'

They claimed the notes I offered and removed themselves from my presence.

'I do not want to see you until rent day, do you hear? When I will gladly recover my three hundred pounds.'

Once they were gone, I kicked Hindley to check if he was likely to stir presently, but he was as senseless as the pyre he lied on. I leaned in to determine his breath, and I was struck by the stench of him. He was near-death, I was certain; I knew the reek of a body rotting from the inside. I had often imagined how I would destroy Hindley, the fight that would be the end of one of us. But I did not mourn the blows that would never come. Hindley's self-degradation suited me – in three years he had aged at least ten.

I looked up when Joseph appeared at the door, uttering curses. *He* was unchanged.

'Be gone! Go to your work. Leave Hindley to me,' I said.

'And Hareton, wat to do w'ith lad?'

I did not answer immediately, for in truth, I had not considered the boy. Hareton was no longer a baby, but what would possess Nelly to leave him there? I could not fathom it. My mind slipped again, to a lifetime ago when I caught Hareton as he fell from Hindley's arms, and from there to the *Othello* when I held the slave-baby aloft before...

'Bring Hareton to me,' I said, gripping the card table. 'We'll soon discover if he will grow as crooked as his father.'

When Joseph turned to leave, I released my hold on the table and straightened my fingers.

'Joseph,' I said, calling him back. He glared at me from the doorway.

'How long has Cathy been at the Grange?' I asked, pausing as the meaning of the question burnt in me like ice. 'How long has she been a Linton?'

'Six month,' he said. 'She took ill after yah ran away, and wud nay depart th' Heights. But Hindley's ungodliness soon put an end tu that, and I pray th' Linton boy has made her pious, or she shal nay scape burnin for eternity.'

'Out of my sight,' I said, enraged. 'You are a hypocrite, Joseph.'

I reached for a table leg situated near the insensible Hindley, being the nearest missile I could grasp, and flung it at Joseph's head. It missed, and he vacated the room roaring damnation at me.

I would discover if I was damned in time, for what would be the purpose of enduring without her? All I had suffered – the humiliation, the cruelty, the debasement of my soul – was all for nothing. Everything I did, such acts that would appal the devil, I did for her. And to what end? My education, the wealth I had acquired, all of it was meaningless unless I shared it with her.

I left Hindley and stormed through the Heights, opening doors and windows, my face wet with hot tears. The furniture was unchanged – the table in the kitchen where Nelly attempted to school me, the chair in which Earnshaw breathed his last and Hindley sat cradling his new wife, the steps on which we listened and should still be worn smooth by the weight of our disobedience – but as I flew from room to room, the house was empty of her.

There was no trace that she had ever existed.

There were days when we escaped from the Heights and hid in the heather until they ceased their searching and let us be. When only the cry of the grouse disturbed the quiet, we knew we were safe: we perched on the edge of Penistone Cragg, out in the open, our feet kicking the air, daring each other to jump. She said it would be our soul's flight: that our spirits would meet in the wind and be carried across the moors; that we would be free of Hindley's tyranny and Joseph's homilies. I remembered the oath we made in the fairy cave – her nerve as she pushed herself through the narrow passageway, unafraid and vowing to never forsake me.

I believed her.

But I was a fool to carry this image of us as fetterless yet joined, slaves to each other yet ungoverned by God, man, even nature. I dared the devil himself to separate us.

I bore this idea, nurtured it, and welcomed it. She said our souls were twined like two oaks, that we could never be uprooted.

But she was a liar. I knew my own destiny – it was ingrained in the Cragg itself, and it was as implacable as the rocks beneath it. I was fated to love my deceiver, my destroyer. How could I not?

Now she was beyond these hills in that palace we once peered at and mocked before she became its inhabitant. Was she content there, in that glass prison with the windows that were stuck fast against the moors, against me?

Why did she choose that mawkish coward over me? She chose empty flattery and fleeting adoration over a love that would outlast these hills, outlast these rocks, and outlast every generation of Lintons still to come. How could she do it?

How could she betray her own heart?

I remained in Wuthering Heights that evening. Hindley, whose wits had dulled in the three years of my absence, was remarkably consoled by the settling of his most immediate gambling debts, and did not bar the door against his enemy, as perhaps he should have.

I handed him a bottle with one hand and took control of the Heights with the other. If he wished to drink himself to death, then I would provide him with the means to do so, and Hareton, who had *her* eyes, I would use as diabolically as his father had used me.

I took my rest in Cathy's old chamber, for it was the only room in the house that still felt haunted by her. She did not take the box-bed with her to the Grange, and when I slid back the panels, I was overcome with a despair I had not known since my weeks in the Tower, for the sheets were slept-in, her books were still piled on the ledge, and the oak in the yard still beat its branch against the casement.

I shut myself in and traced the carving on the ledge until my finger stiffened and the sky lightened.

Catherine Earnshaw.

Catherine Heathcliff.

Catherine Linton.

When morning came it arrived slowly, emerging over the edge of the moor like a realisation. I watched the sun's advance as it illuminated the earth by inchmeal, waking the lapwings in the heather first and then the plovers in the copse at the far end of the farm. Yesterday's rain had left its footprints on the land — pools of water as clear as mirrors and beyond, a country of mud and marsh and moil.

When the sun's light reached the window I placed the pistol in my satchel, hiding it amongst the papers that would make me master of Wuthering Heights if Cathy still loved me. If she had changed beyond all recognition, then Hindley could rot in this damned house.

I left Cathy's chamber with the impress of her name, in all its manifestations, tapping the casement before my eyes.

Catherine Earnshaw

Catherine Heathcliff

Catherine Linton

Catherine Heathcliff

With my mind untethered, I descended to the kitchen, where Hindley was waiting for me. His eyes, although deep set with black crescents underneath them, were unclouded.

'You are awake,' I said, sitting at the table so that we faced one another. I blinked the myriad Catherines away.

'Aye,' he said, averting his gaze, for he was holding a tankard of whiskey.

'But not for long,' I said, letting my eyes rest on his liquor.

'Then let me speak plainly before you are beyond reason. As you are aware, I have paid some of your smaller gambling debts. From our brief conversation yesterday, it seems there are still many larger debts that must be paid to safeguard your life.'

Hindley had ceased listening. His eyes began to close, and his head swayed, too heavy for his neck. I snatched the tankard from him and threw its contents in his face. How I wanted to set a match to him.

'Now do I have your attention?' I asked.

Hindley nodded pitifully.

'This is what will happen,' I continued. 'If I return from Thrushcross Grange revived – yes, I plan to visit *her* – then I will purchase Wuthering Heights for two thousand pounds. That sum should substantially cover all your debts, including those owed to the bank. I will have a Gimmerton solicitor draw up a contract, which you *will* sign.'

'Why? Why would you help me?' he asked, his speech slurred.

I smiled at this misunderstanding of my character.

'You are family,' I said, and remembering the Shakespeare play I once saw, I added, 'I forgive your rankest faults, Hindley. All of them.'

He was too addled to grasp the irony in my words and attempted to take my hand.

It was as distasteful to me as the hand of a slave in New Speke would be, but I grasped it, despite its clammy coldness and the repulsion which rose in my throat.

I withdrew my hand quickly, but Hindley seemed satisfied by my show of friendship.

'I will leave you now,' I said.

'When will you return?'

'This evening. I have taken the key to the kitchen door; there is no need to wait up for me,' I explained. 'Tomorrow, during your brief hours of wakefulness, I will present you with the contract. In the meantime, Joseph will commence searching for the deeds of Wuthering Heights.'

I turned to leave, but I had forgotten about Hareton.

'As for your son, he is *my* ward now. *I* will complete his education.'

But Hindley's mind had already drifted. He lay his head on the table and embraced his empty tankard like a lover.

If Cathy did not greet me with pleasure, with the vehemence of old, I would smother Hindley in his stupor and turn my murderer's hands on myself.

It would be a kindness to us both.

I met no one on the walk to Thrushcross Grange.

The moors were saturated by yesterday's deluge and best avoided by those unfamiliar with its hidden paths. The solitude suited me, for my thoughts were company enough.

I remembered how I ran these paths with Cathy, who would sometimes stray into the mire and lose her boots, but she would always run on, barefoot. I had thrown myself blindly down one of these tracks on the night I left, arriving in Gimmerton with the storm at my back and barely a sketch of a plan.

Sense dictated that I should be on my horse, and on the road, but there was something seemly about venturing on this journey by foot, something symbolic. I was returned, and it seemed fitting that it should be the moors that delivered me to Cathy.

I slowed when I saw the neat line of poplars, the cultivated lawn and the gravel footpath that led to the back of Thrushcross Grange. It was mere ornament. How could Cathy endure it?

I edged toward the trees and hid in the walled garden, concealing myself in the dappled darkness of the blossoms. It was nearly dusk, for the moon had climbed over the garden wall and the shadows had lengthened. Where had I been for all this time? When I left, it was morning, I was sure of it.

I lurked in the garden for an hour, or so I thought; I was not sure if I could trust my senses. There was an appalling weight on my chest that I could not dislodge. When a light finally appeared in the window above the kitchen, I took my chance and made for the porch.

A woman carried a basket of apples from the orchard – a sight that startled me, for up until that moment the garden was as still as death. She stopped at the door to the kitchen and set her burden on the lower step, taking her rest, and looking up at the moon, which was full and hazy against the dimming sky.

I recognised her bearing; she was dressed as a servant, but her haughtiness betrayed her identity. I wanted to embrace her, to tell her everything, to beg her to let me in. But I did not have time.

She lifted her bundle and was about to enter the house when I emerged from the shadows of the porch, startling her.

She froze, her face waxen.

'You do not know me?' I asked. 'Look,' I said, lifting my face to the light from the kitchen window, 'I am no stranger.'

The apples tumbled from her basket like little heads and rolled to meet me.

I stepped forward, crushing one beneath my boot, and stood tall.

Acknowledgments

I am grateful for the support and encouragement of the Manchester Writing School MMU, notably Gregory Norminton and Nicholas Royle. They steered the first versions of this novel, and without their enthusiasm for the book, you wouldn't be holding it now.

Thank you to Aderyn Press, for trusting in this novel and releasing it into the world. Thank you to Kari Brownlie for the inspired cover design. Thank you to Julia Forster, publicist extraordinaire, for championing this novel.

I am immensely fortunate in my editor, Rebecca John, whose careful eye and discernment are evident throughout the novel. I'm not sure what I did to deserve Rebecca, but I am immensely grateful for her.

Thank you to my early readers and first supporters: Hayley Blackwell, Jane Love, Tracey Rees-Cooke and Dr Fiona Cameron.

Special thanks to Ms Elaine Jones and Mrs Beth Wennell, the former for telling me that I 'simply must be a writer', and the latter for introducing me, properly, to Wuthering Heights. I hope you both approve of the outcome.

The following books were invaluable during the writing of this novel: *Liverpool As It Was 1775 to 1800* by Richard Brooke, 1853 (Liverpool Libraries and Information Service, reprinted in 2003); *A Slaver's Log Book by Captain Theophilus Conneau, 1853* (Robert Hale Limited, printed in 1977); *The Slave Trade: The History of the Atlantic Slave Trade 1440-1870*, Hugh Thomas

(Picador, 1997); *The Fine Art of Smuggling: King's Cutters vs. Smugglers: 1700-1855*, E. Keble Chatterton (Fireship Press, 2008). Emily Brontë's Wuthering Heights was the inspiration for this novel, or more specifically, the 'spaces' in her narrative. I hope I have inhabited these spaces well.

My love and immense thanks to my mam and dad, Gillian and Wayne Roberts, whose belief in me has never wavered.

Finally, this novel would still be in a drawer were it not for the persistence and care of my husband, Glyn. Thank you for everything, from the biannual, sometimes triannual, research trips to Haworth to the extra bedtime stories so that I could 'just write another 300 words'. This book is dedicated to you.

Biography

Nicola Edwards is a PhD candidate at the University of Bangor and teaches English and Classics in a school in North Wales. Nicola has worked as a journalist and has lectured on race and representation in the media for Race Council Wales. Her non-fiction writing has appeared in Wales Arts Review. *This Thing of Darkness*, her first novel, won the Michael Schmidt Prize at the Manchester Writing School.